SOMETHING
WENT
COLD

SOMETHING WENT COLD

GLENN RESCHKE

atmosphere press

TABLE OF CONTENTS

To the Brothers Grimm, Aesop and Shakespeare for great stories that have educated, entertained and enthralled.

#METOO

With a grunt and a shudder, he finished and withdrew himself from her. He mumbled something cheerful as he clumsily bounded from the bed, tossing a condom into the silver meshed wastebasket next to the bed. He reached down to grab his underwear before positioning it with a snap. The girl anticipated his bending over to pick up his clothes thrown askew on her bedroom floor and quickly averted her eyes to be spared the sight of a 280-pound middle-aged man's split buttocks. She slithered off the silk sheets and grabbed a stick of gum and a few breath mints off the night-stand adjacent her king-size bed and hastily threw them in her mouth.

After throwing on a Kiryu silk robe, she silently opened a small drawer on the night-stand and snagged an alcohol wipe to rub over her feminine areas and just as quickly discarded it into the wire mesh pail. She sat with her back to him deliberately and read something on her smartphone but it was busywork to fill the time.

"I do enjoy you. You're the highlight of my week," he offered while searching for his yellow linen dress shirt.

She forced a polite smile in response while pulling her black hair into a ponytail. *Just pay me already.* As if he read her thoughts, he reached into his suit coat jacket that

3

rested on her office chair directly opposite a modular black computer station and took a wad of bills from a tan leather wallet.

He fingered the wad of bills with a flourish. "Here's one thousand dollars as agreed. And a tip!"

"Thank you," she replied robotically.

He sank heavily into her computer chair and pulled his socks on, then his dress shoes.

"No shoes inside the house."

"Aww, come on! I'm one of your best customers," he said in a sharper tone.

"No shoes."

His eyes scanned her hoping to see a glint of wavering in her angular face. Finding none, he neatly laid aside his polished Florsheims.

"Your wish is my command, my lady."

He spied his tie hanging promiscuously from one of the faux metallic sconces in the hallway adjacent the bedroom and after retrieving it, began twirling it like a cabaret girl on a Vegas stage.

Just leave already. She didn't want conversation or company; she wanted it over as soon as possible, and most of all, she wanted the money. Her ideal client would arrive promptly, undress, thrust, finish, pay, dress, leave—and all without talking. It was a hard façade to maintain: be likable enough so they come back without inviting infatuation.

"You're not much of a talker, are you? I've been here like ten times and you've hardly said a word to me. And I don't think I've seen you smile ever," the client said matter-of-factly.

She moved the gum and mints to the other side of her

mouth and forced a slippery smile.

"I got a lot on my mind. Sick mother and all. Cancer," she lied.

Surprise filled his face as he buttoned his shirt.

"That's the first time you've ever shared anything personal."

He pulled his sport coat over his arms and pulled it down a number of times as it was too small for his corpulent frame. Most would find comedy in the way he donned and tugged the jacket, but not her.

A dog's growl mingled with a kitten's plaintive plea echoed from the ground below, catching the attention of the client. As he slid the screen door open and walked onto the balcony to investigate, an involuntary gasp escaped his lips: a pit bull had a small kitten in its mouth. Across the parking lot watching were two muscular, heavily tattooed, twenty-something Hispanic men in white, wife-beater tank tops and red bandanas sitting atop Ducati motorcycles in the open-air parking stalls.

With a hiss and screech, the kitten's mother jumped on the dog's back and dug its teeth and claws into the pit bull's neck. The dog pushed off the cat with its right paw and clamped down on its neck then wrung the cat violently to the left and the right, snapping its neck. The kitten lay a few feet from its mother, its delicate body broken. The kitten's agonized mewling caught the attention of the dog who pitilessly seized the kitten's head into its gaping jaws before snapping the neck.

The sound of clapping disturbed the client's gaze. He flashed a glance at the dead cats below and watched as the dog bounded proudly toward its masters.

"That was brutal," the client said, closing the sliding

door behind him. "That poor kitten. Something so innocent treated so brutally."

The girl rose off the bed and peeped carefully through the screen door. She recognized the men as tenants of the four-plex adjacent hers. They sometimes whistled at her from their second-floor balcony when seeing her in the parking lot. She watched the older of the two tear off a piece of its burger and toss it to the dog sitting on the ground in front of them.

"That's the way it goes," she coolly responded, sitting back down.

Spying his belt in the corner, the client retrieved it and slide it through his pant loops in silence.

"You're kind of cold-blooded, aren't you?"

There was no reason to respond. The client had long thought she didn't like people or animals or children or air. Now he was sure of it.

He hesitated a moment then reached into his jacket for his wallet and pulled out another one hundred dollar bill and placed it gently on the computer desk.

"For your mom."

He picked up his dress shoes with his left hand and strolled heavily down the stairs. *Finally*. She waited until she heard the door click close then shot down the steps, accidentally clipping one of the terra-cotta planters at the foot of the staircase. She lost her balance and hit the wall where the only painting in the apartment hung, now askew. Expletives fouled her lips, but it did little to assuage the pain. Limping to the entrance-way, she turned the deadbolt to lock and before ascending the stairs, carefully straightened the painting. It was an unremarkable representation of a 19th-century clipper ship in a storm-tossed sea. The ship had a square rig and three masts full with wind while white foam splashed over its bow. No land or safe harbor could be seen, only gray, uneven sea. One sailor was on the ship's deck—alone—and that's why she bought it. After ensuring there was no unwanted dirt on the carpet, she traversed the staircase, holding onto the black metallic railing.

She would shower as was her habit after every client visit. Afterward, she donned her all-black running clothes, and plaited her hair but not before concealing a small two-toned, three-inch Swiss Army knife in a black leather holder on her left bicep. While adjusting her ear plugs as she exited her apartment, a thirty-something neighbor ambled past her on the sidewalk with a leashed Labrador and a baby stroller. Disgust crossed the woman's face. *She knows what I do, but who cares.* The girl then wrapped the Velcro on a hand-held water bottle around her left hand and started the timer on her black sports watch.

She quickly settled into a comfortable pace while songs of a famous Latin pop singer played in her ears. Overhead the Egyptian blue of the East Bay sky was dissolving into midnight black. The heat of the day had broken, leaving the air windless and tinged with the faint smell of aerosolized eucalyptus from the trees lining her middle-class suburb. She wound her way through the rows of houses and streets leading to her preferred trail. She didn't like running through the neighborhood streets as they reminded her of what she never had. She tilted her head upward and focused on the trees as she passed manicured lawns and yew hedges fronting middle-class homes with amber lights glinting through bay windows, behind which, in her imagination, happy families lived.

Running was her escape. Her mind often drifted to her childhood when she was the warrior-maiden engaged in imaginary sword fights with great soldiers and dragons. Her favorite game, she remembered, was outrunning a pesky Chihuahua on the block opposite her family home. She would roll past its house on her bike and wait for it to yap and growl as it pursued her down the street. She learned quickly that the predators in real life were not as easily outrun. Soon after her father died, her mother re-married. Her step-father at first was kind and loving. She would come home from school and he would play with her and give her dolls and candy bars and whisper in her ear, "Don't tell your mama. This is our little secret, okay?"

"Okay!" She would smile back with all the innocence of a child.

Indifference and hopelessness were lessons she would soon learn. The step-father began visiting her bedroom late at night to teach her "big people games." She learned other adult things, too, such as how suffering is endurance, and how the soul craves justice like an addict a fix.

She would go to her mother with a tear-stained face pleading for protection but there would be none. Pleasure-seeking filled her mother's and step-father's time leaving her ever alone. There were no relatives or other family members to visit. They had long ago cut ties with her mother, and her dead father's relatives showed no interest in her. Her only companion was the family dog, Shatzi, a small, all-black Shih Tzu ever abundant in affection and the only unconditional love she would experience in her childhood.

Upon her constant rejection of the step-father's late-night advances, he threatened he would kill her beloved Shatzi if she didn't give in to him. There was a part of her that didn't believe him; her childlike purity made her believe no one could be so monstrous. Any remaining innocence in her heart drained away when her step-father snapped the dog's neck in front of her. In a childhood filled with tears, that was the last time she wept.

The visits stopped at fourteen. A few years thereafter, her mother told her that after she graduated high school, she was on her own.

When she turned eighteen, the girl moved out and took a job as a waitress in a local diner. In the fall, she enrolled at Diablo Valley Community College with the goal of transferring to UC Berkeley and then perhaps nursing school. In the summers and holiday breaks, she worked numerous extra shifts to make money for school and took a second and third job. She eventually saved enough to buy a fifteen-year-old, two-door economy car. The girl was poor but free from her mother and step-father—and for the first time, from fear.

Her part-time waitressing jobs coupled with school loans and grants allowed the girl to live adequately, but there was no money for luxuries the other students talked about, like weekend trips to Yosemite or summer vacations to Europe.

Her trips were limited to the numerous hiking trails dotting the Bay Area. Though a heavily populated region, some hikes gave the impression of utter solitude. Such hikes were her religion, her peace.

Poverty and the stress of bitter experience can hone, refine. It can inflame ambition and so it did in the girl. She devoted herself to her schooling and was an excellent student—except for math.

Written in an unmistakable red marker, a D+ adorned the top right of her latest Algebra test along with a cryptic note from the professor to see him after class. After the other students emptied out, she timidly made her way to the professor's desk.

"You wanted to see me, Professor?"

"Let's talk in my office," he replied.

After he closed the door of his office, he slung his coat on a small table next to a bookcase filled with books and magazines scattered askew on its shelves. Out of place on the lowest shelf were a few bottles of mouthwash and paper bags.

"Please. Sit down," he offered, motioning toward one of the two empty chairs facing his desk. She gingerly sat on the edge of the cheap, metallic chair found only in garage sales and unzipped her black spring coat. The professor took a step back toward the windows and turned the Venetian blind's vertical wand, closing the windows. He sat on the ledge adjacent to the window and after resuming eye contact with the girl began rubbing his genitalia.

"You're a pretty girl with a very womanly figure."

"What's this about?" she coughed out.

"How would you like an A grade in this class?"

She knew what the offer would be and bolted upright, fumbling nervously with the zipper on her coat.

"No," she replied firmly.

"I know you want to go to Berkeley. You need this class to satisfy your generals. As it is, you're barely at a D level— and that's if I'm charitable. I'll give you an A and even write you a letter of recommendation. It'll be a one-time thing."

"I can't do that," she said quietly.

"You don't even need to take your clothes off. What I have in mind won't require that," he said without the slightest tone of persuasion in his voice.

Her step-father never had any interest in that. He would sodomize or penetrate her but never that. *I don't know if I can.* But she needed to pass; she needed to get into Berkeley. Desperation filled her soul as she wrestled with cascading emotion.

"I get an A. And a letter of recommendation. And it's a one-time thing," she said, her voice breaking.

The whiff of compromise emboldened him. "Yes. I'll even throw in a quick hundred dollars as a bonus."

The professor was true to his word, and not long afterward she received a lucrative proposition from an attractive older man while working the late-night shift at one of the local diners close to campus. The professor had recommended her, he said. She was repulsed but relented with the offer of a staggering one thousand dollars plus tip—if she pleased him. Word spread and within a few weeks, she had a forty-to-fifty-five-year-old clientele and an income far surpassing three waitressing jobs. She limited her moral compromising to the breaking of the seventh commandment, avoiding alcohol and drugs the way she avoided step-fathers.

The girl pushed the volume button down on the music device as she turned left onto the road that led to the eastern entrance of Briones Regional Park. The nauseating effluvium of horse manure hung in the air, but it soon passed as she snaked her way toward the parkland's hiking trails.

The scenery quickly changed as one neared the park, serving as a stark contrast to the densely populated area surrounding it. Multi-trunked California bays, big-leaf maples, and oak trees shaded the park's paths, intermingling with a wide array of diverse plant life dotting the countryside, including sagebrush, brambles, coyote brush, and the occasional California coffeeberry. Significant animal life also resided in the rolling hills and earthy brush of the park. Coyotes were commonly seen, as were red-tailed hawks who patrolled its skies for groundhogs and squirrels. Numerous trailheads twisted their way into the woodland and were a popular choice among local hikers and joggers.

Passing through the unmanned guard shack at the entrance to the graveled parking lot, she noticed the green entry gate was open. This was unusual but the girl ignored it. *It's nice not having to unhinge and close it for once,* she thought.

She ran through to the Alhambra Creek Trail southwest until it turned dramatically north and upward, becoming the Spengler Trail. A mile or so away was its termination point, marked conveniently by another green cow fence where she turned around.

Nearing the descent of the hill that led to the Alhambra Creek Trail, the girl heard the steady off-key bleating of a police siren and roar of multiple motorcycles jetting up the trail. And gunshots. She took the earbuds out of her ears and slung them around her neck the way a doctor would a stethoscope, then made her way into a clearing that led to an overlook of the trail. There, she quietly sequestered herself behind a wall of brambles that served as a natural camouflage.

As she crouched to her haunches, the two Hispanic men from the four-plex next to her building came into view. They were speeding parallel each other down the trail with one of them carrying a black duffel bag over his shoulder. Two hundred yards behind them, a single California Highway Patrolman followed. In unison, they shot rapid-fire toward the patrolman causing him to fishtail and skid uncontrollably before crashing into the brush fifty yards before the intersection of the trail. The girl could faintly hear his curses as she watched him take cover behind the bike. After one of the shots, a loud metallic clang caused the motorcycle's police lights and siren to fail. She watched the patrolman desperately try to radio for help before flinging away the corded microphone in frustration, only to have it recoil and hit him in the face. She suppressed a chuckle.

The brothers came to a screeching halt before the northerly turn of the trail. They hastily re-loaded their handguns while speaking in rapid-fire Spanish.

"*Tengo un idea*," she heard the bigger of the brothers say, then watched as he sped off past the Alhambra Creek Trail and continue easterly on the Spengler. *Smart move*. A rush of fear coursed through her as she saw the other brother gun the motorcycle up the hill.

The roar of the Ducati filled the trail as he raced upward. The sun was close to setting and with the natural camouflage of the environment she was sure she wouldn't be seen. To her horror, he veered sharply ten yards from her, engaged the kick stand and jumped off.

A number of oak trees lined the trail and with the abundance of prickly brushes, it discouraged anyone from wandering too deeply into the wood. He nervously glanced around the area. *"Perfecto,"* she heard him whisper.

She breathlessly watched him push the bag into a vertical split of black earth slightly downhill from her position then cover it with leaves and dirt. Even from her vantage point, the hiding place was barely visible.

He nervously looked around a moment before straddling his Ducati and pealing down the hill. He accelerated past the Alhambra Creek Trail and then east on the same trail his brother used. As the roar of the motorcycle diminished with distance, the girl threw a glance at the patrolman as he took off limping toward the trailhead.

Taking a deep guzzle from her water bottle, she wiped the sweat off her forehead, then lighted from her hiding spot. With each footfall, loud crunching noises from the dead leaves could be heard as she stepped toward the bag's hiding spot. She set aside the water bottle and easily unearthed the bag, then unzipped it.

She gasped.

It was filled with ten thousand dollar bundles, and incongruously, a pair of black baseball batting gloves. She dug her hand deep into the bag and each time withdrew identical stacks. *Drug money.*

It took only a few hurried moments to count it—it totaled six million dollars. Euphoria and ecstasy crowded her emotions as her mind began to race. *They're coming back, and soon.* She realized the police, too, would be arriving as well, and they would comb the area for evidence. The easiest route would be to go back through the Alhambra Creek Trail parking lot. *Too stupid.* The longest route would be to hike six miles through the park to the Bear Creek trail, then another seven miles around the park to her apartment. Or, she could traverse the hills, off trail. In the dark.

There was also the risk of the environment. Coyotes frequented the area—she had seen them herself numerous times. Cows also grazed freely on the rolling hills and often rested on the trails, to the irritation of hikers and mountain bikers, and while harmless, could be formidable when spooked. She also remembered reports of a mountain lion last spring in the northern reach of the park not far from her. Various snakes also patrolled the grounds among the ubiquitous poison ivy and sharp brambles that littered the foliage. And nightfall was fast approaching.

Emotions short-circuited her logic. She needed a plan. *Think it through.* The easy decision would be to leave the money and take just a few of the bundles. She could put them down her yoga pants atop her genitalia and jog out the same way she came. That would be manageable, safe.

No. She wanted it all. *It's worth the risk.* The girl took a deep swig of her water bottle as a fresh cool breeze swirled about her. She had an epiphany: a line may have to be crossed. The thought didn't trouble her. She felt her resolve growing within her—she would leave this wood with the money or die here. An unexpected feeling of comfort followed. She could not—would not—turn away from this chance. Money would make her free to do whatever she wanted for the rest of her life. Another realization came: it would all be over soon no matter what the outcome.

The girl carefully delineated each of the plan's steps in her mind. She would run through the park to the Bear Creek entrance area, find a hiding place for the money, and run the seven or so miles back to her apartment. There were shorter routes with the Briones Road parking lot a mere two miles away, but that would be too predictable. The police would be involved soon enough, too. Key to the plan was invisibility—she could not be seen with the money, either by the police or the brothers. To pull this off, she needed to be inconspicuous and unpredictable. It would be odd to see a woman running at night, especially along Alhambra Creek Road, but not enough to draw attention. Her endurance and courage would be called upon this night.

She re-tied her shoes and quickly re-stretched her legs before slinging the duffel bag around her left shoulder. It was heavier than expected. But she didn't care—she had her plan.

It would be around midnight when she got home. She would shower, eat, and sleep till 3:30 A.M. Then, she would drive to the hiding spot she'd select and retrieve the bag. It would still be early and she could most likely sneak the money into her apartment. No, she couldn't take the gamble of being seen with the bag. Instead, she would drive to the Waterfront Park Softball Field on Joe DiMaggio Drive near downtown Martinez and sleep a few hours. Other than the occasional homeless person meandering about, only a city worker charged with managing the softball fields would come through, and the girl would already be gone. Worst case scenario: the city worker would tell her to leave and if so, she would feign homelessness and drive away.

Around 8:00 A.M., the girl would arise and eat breakfast at the dingy restaurant across from the apartments adjacent Diablo Valley College. After eating, she would drive to the Trader Joe's grocery store in nearby Concord and shop, and then to the church catty-corner to it. The parking lot at the church, the girl knew, had significant tree cover and privacy. The girl would empty the bags of food in her trunk, fill them halfway with money, then top them with groceries. It would take ten minutes at most to do the transfer, she estimated. If someone would be there, she'd simply drive back to the softball field and do it there. If everything went according to plan, she would drive home from the church and take the grocery bags into the apartment. To the casual onlooker, it would just be a young woman carrying groceries after shopping. *It's a good plan. Simple. Unobtrusive. Careful.*

The girl would have to carry the bag the entire six miles through the park—in the dark—and sequester it somewhere on the road for quick retrieval. She knew no park worker manned the entrance gate to any of the trailheads except for weekends. She should be alone in the park when she hid the bag. *This will be the most difficult part.*

The blare of motorcycles faintly resounded in the distance. A moment later, two gunshots echoed through the park.

The two brothers dragged the dead policeman's body to the bathroom on the Orchard Trail just off the Alhambra Creek trailhead entrance. They sat him on the toilet and tied rope around his waist, securing him to the white porcelain water tank. The older brother secured the patrolman's feet in front of the bowl then closed the door and climbed over the stall partition.

"He shouldn't be discovered until tomorrow morning at the earliest," the older brother said in Spanish.

"Good idea. Now let's get the money," the younger brother smirked.

"After we get it, we've got to leave through another parking lot. If he called it in, they'll come looking for him. And soon."

Night had fallen over the park, which only amplified the roar of the motorcycles as they raced up the trail. As the younger passed the dead patrolman's bike, he flashed a middle finger at it and mumbled, "*Hijo de puta.*"

They veered hard right up the Spengler Trail hill then again to the overlook.

"It's pay day!" the younger brother whooped as he bounded from his bike.

The older brother sat on his bike and lighted a cigarette while the younger made his way through the thick brambles that were almost as dark as the night. He heard leaves thrown about then the sound of hands moving through earth and leaves.

"It's not here!" the younger brother shouted in a panic.

"What do you mean it's not there, idiot?" he said playfully as he drew a deep drag from his cigarette.

"It's not here! It's not here! This is the spot I *know* it is!" The panic in his voice jolted the older brother. He jumped off his bike and moved through the brush menacingly as the bike fell heavily to the earth.

"This is not a joke—do you understand me? Where is it?" he said as he leaned over and grabbed his younger brother by the neck.

"I swear this is where I put it. I swear it. I stopped here on purpose as I thought it was a perfect spot: just up the hill, really hidden, all these bushes, this hole. Bro, I *know* this is the spot. I know it!"

Even in the dark, the older brother could see the honesty in his younger brother's eyes. A surge of panic hit him. He let go of his younger brother's neck and raised himself. A beat passed before he threw his cigarette to the ground and smashed it with his left foot.

"Come with me."

The older brother picked up his bike and activated the kickstand. As he leaned against the seat, he folded his bulging arms. The younger brother ran his hands through his hair repeatedly as he paced, cursing.

"Someone's been here. Someone saw you hide the money. Less than half an hour has passed since you hid it and that means they're close," the older brother said, thinking aloud.

"This is a nightmare, man," the younger replied, almost whimpering.

"What would you do if you just found a bag full of money?"

"I don't know!"

"This is why I run this business, little brother—you don't think," he said, almost shouting. "Think! He had to have seen you put the money in that hole to find it. And if he saw you put the money there, he saw what went down with the cop. He was too close not to. Which means he wouldn't leave through the closest gate, as it would be too dangerous."

"He wouldn't go out the same way he came in?"

"No, because he would know we'd be coming back soon to get it, and the closest exit point is Alhambra Creek, that way," he said, pointing in its direction.

"But what if he was hiding when we came in and killed the cop? Then he could've just left when we went past him," the younger brother asked.

"Did you see a car when we came back in?"

"I wasn't looking! He could've been hiding!" he replied angrily.

"Yes, but you're missing the point. There was no car or bike, which means it's a jogger or a hiker. Probably a jogger as nobody hikes here when it's dark," said the older brother, pursing his lips.

"There are other entrances, too. The Briones Road one is only two miles away."

"No, no. It's got to be a jogger who came in through the Alhambra Creek entrance. No one is going to go this deep into the park at night from Briones Road."

He always sees all the angles, thought the younger brother.

"He wants to avoid us," he continued as he rubbed his arms for warmth in the growing evening chill, "Which means either going up the hills and into the brush...or toward another exit. And he won't go up the hills because he knows even in this dark, with the moonlight we could see him."

"The other trailhead entrance has to be least five or six miles away."

"Yes, and that's where he's going."

"What do we do when we find him?"

"I think you know." The other brother smirked, putting on his helmet. "After we take him down, and get the money, we push his body off the trail and cover it. The smell of the dead body should attract coyotes and maybe the police will think it was an animal attack. Then we go through the closest exit."

"Good plan," the younger brother said, turning the key of his ignition.

The sound of a motorcycle again pierced the air. Then another, causing the girl to quicken her pace. She was making good time but knew she was a long way from the Bear Creek entrance. She stopped a moment and turned toward the sound, wiping sweat from her brow. The sound of the bikes was getting closer. *They're coming this way.*

She'd thought of this possibility. About twenty yards ahead, she spied a large oak with a v-shaped crotch recess about ten feet from the ground. The tree's overhanging limbs combined with the height of the crotch would be a perfect hiding place.

Time was against her. She had to scale the tree with the bag and get back on the trail before they came down the slight rise in the trail. Approaching the tree, she spied an oblong cavity six feet above the ground on the tree's left side and a knob about the same height but below the crotch. She braced her left foot against it and secured her right hand on the knob. Then, with her right-hand pulling and her left leg pushing, the girl propelled herself upward. She rested on her left forearm while sliding the bag off her back into the opening then reversed the process. In a moment she was back on the trail just before the motorbikes roared over the rise.

The girl cursed under her breath. Retrieving it later in the early morning hours would require another significant jaunt into the park—and out again. With any luck they would go past her. She gulped hard as the roar of the bikes closed upon her.

The younger brother's bike screamed past her ten yards before he banked hard right, causing him to skid to a stop directly in front of her. The older brother slid to a stop behind her at almost the same instant. Be casual, the girl thought to herself, as she buried her face and brow into the crook of her right arm to wipe the sweat from her forehead and cheeks.

"You have something that's ours," the older brother said as he took off his helmet.

"What are you talking about?" the girl said turning and putting her hands on her hips. "I'm training for a marathon and this is the only time the park's empty. You do know bikes are not allowed in here?" she finished with feigned irritation.

"Running at night through the park! Lying bitch," the younger brother said as he lighted from his bike. He took out a handgun from somewhere in the bike's dashboard and then let the bike fall to the ground.

Behind her, the older brother dismounted and with his right heel, booted the kickstand into place. He took a threatening step toward her.

"Tell us where it is now! Make it easy on us and we'll give you a couple of bundles for your trouble. Then we'll go on our way," he said, almost gentlemanly.

She glanced at the younger brother impeding her path. He repeatedly rubbed the muzzle of the gun on his thigh as if to scratch an itch. Her heartbeat pounded so hard she could feel it in her throat.

For a moment, she was a little girl again, bullied and powerless. *No more.*

"Well?"

The girl drew a deep breath as a scowl formed on her face. "Screw you, *puta*."

Surprise flashed across the older brother's face for a moment before he leaned his upper body to the right and unloaded a blow deep into her stomach. The girl groaned as she fell to the ground. She instinctively wrapped her arms around her torso to cope with the pain, gasping for air as shock and fear throttled through her.

"I'll bet you're not so cocky now, are you!" laughed the younger brother.

"If you kill me, you'll never find it. Ever," she said, haltingly as she gasped for air.

"Last chance. Where's the money?" the older brother hissed.

"As soon as I tell you, you'll kill me."

A kick in the ribs from the younger brother brought a new shock of pain.

"How do you know we won't kill you now? We already killed that cop," said the younger proudly.

The older brother's kick almost broke a rib; she knew she had to act. Her mind raced for options as the pain and fear coursed through her.

"When you heard us coming, that's probably when you hid the money, which means it's close by," the older brother said, rubbing his neck and chin.

The brothers began speaking in their native tongue. The girl listened carefully to see if she could hear anything of use. She didn't have to wait long. The younger brother carefully enunciated the phrase *mátala ahora*—kill her now—as if he wanted her to understand. As she listened, the rage grew, sharpening her will to a fine point as the argument between the brothers intensified.

It was the distraction she needed. While cradling her torso, she planted her forehead on the ground and twisted so she faced downward with her hands out of sight. She quietly moved her right arm from the elbow down to unsheathe the blade in its holster on her left bicep. It slid out soundlessly. She feigned a cough to suppress any sound of the knife unfurling, securing it firmly in her right hand.

The brothers were shouting and gesticulating wildly now. Suddenly, the younger brother leaned down and grabbed her by the hair with his left hand, yanking her torso upward. He then buried the gun's muzzle into her left temple.

"Where is the money, *marica*?" he yelled.

"It's here," seethed the girl.

With her left hand, she parried the gun away from her temple and felt for the trigger. After a quick yank and push of the brother's arm to her right, she fired multiple shots toward the older brother, catching him in his left thigh and stomach. Almost simultaneously she sliced through the younger brother's femoral artery then upward into his genitalia. The younger brother dropped the gun as he fell backward, howling. Breathless, the girl hurriedly grabbed the gun then rolled to her right and shot at the younger brother with two shots in succession. His head exploded outward with a sound reminiscent of watermelon hitting concrete. She then turned and without hesitation, fired at the other brother, hitting him in the right leg.

Shock overcame the older brother. He hastily reached around to his back for his gun but stopped when the girl straddled him.

"Everyone has a plan until they get punched—isn't that

right, *puta*?" the girl said.

"You killed my brother!" the older brother said, mewling.

The girl drew in a deep breath. "Yes," she said, holding the gun the way policewoman do on television.

"Take the money. Take it! Just let me go," he whimpered.

"Keep your hands on your stomach," she said, stepping backward and to her right, away from his body. The blood on his hands and clothing looked like oil in the dark pitch.

"I promise I won't come after you if you'll let me go. I promise!" His groveling tone was a stark contrast to his intimidating appearance.

The girl glanced at the gun then back at him. Emotion and memories crowded upon her, but she stifled it as she always had.

"How does it feel? How does it feel to be bullied? How does it feel to be trapped knowing no matter what you do, you can't escape?"

The brother listened and paused trying to digest the intensity of her remarks before raising his hands and begging for his life. The girl took another step back and lowered the gun while gaming out the situation in her mind. The killing of the other brother would be defensible in a court of law, the girl reasoned. But not if she killed the second. The police would take the money and it would disappear down the black hole of the government and at best she'd get a manslaughter charge—and jail time. The brother took confidence at her body language. Another plea escaped his lips, but it was different than the others. It was a high-pitched wail mixed with emotion that surprised her. The girl aimed carefully, firing a shot into his genitalia. A loud scream pierced the air as he instantly grabbed his genital area with both hands, curling up into a ball.

"How you feeling, *miho*?"

The girl stood still, a silent, dark sentinel, drinking in satisfaction from his grief and pain. Beats passed before she pointed the gun at his forehead and fired. Bone and brain matter shot up and backward before his body slumped to the ground. Blood poured from the wound and mixed with the growing black-colored eddy from the brother's groin into a pool that moved slowly toward her.

The girl lowered the gun and listened. She turned her body to look around but there was no one; the only sound was a small flitting of wind coursing around her and the gravel crackling beneath her feet. A stronger gust brought the smell of the forest as it flicked her pony-tail and caressed her neck. She looked to the west where the dark pink and purple sky fought for dominance with the last embers of daylight. Above, stars could be seen peeping through the clouds. She paused a moment to scan her feelings and being. There was no soul-ripping, no blackness. No coloring of mind or being. No palpable sense of loss. Only something unexpected.

Disgust.

The whimpering and high-pitched wail from someone so physically imposing was unmanly. Another emotion joined the disgust—pleasure. To see justice done, to fight back so decidedly and win, was exhilarating. *I'm the predator now.*

She turned to practical matters, first removing the older brother's bandana and wiping the gun clean. She then stripped the younger brother of his tank top using it to wipe the blood off the blade. After securing the money, the urge to urinate intruded. She slung the duffel bag off her back and onto the trail.

The girl looked at the lifeless bodies askew on the ground and suddenly wished she were male. The thought made her chuckle. Being a female would have to suffice. The girl would not deprive herself of an additional trophy. She removed her yoga pants to her ankles then crouched down and relieved herself on the faces of the dead brothers.

After dragging the bodies into the brush, she deliberately rubbed their faces with dirt and mud before pushing their faces deep into the soft ground to contaminate the urine. As she turned the older brother over, a black gun handle protruded outward from his pants. *This could be useful.* The girl retrieved it, and after ensuring the safety was on, placed it carefully into the bag. She could feel her energy draining rapidly and for the first time doubted she could make it back to her apartment.

A coyote's yowling in the distance shook her out of her reverie. The girl listened to the other sounds about her. The wind rasped through the grass as an owl's cooing mixed with a cow's lowing. The wind ripped through her again, stronger this time. Night had finally come. The girl drained the remaining water from her water bottle and went through her options as an electric tension between exhilaration and fatigue fought for dominance.

The girl glanced at the younger brother's helmet near his fallen motorcycle. She couldn't ride the bike back to her apartment with a duffel bag flung over her back. No one could see the bag—that was fundamental to her plan, she reminded herself. And any association to the bike would inexorably lead back to the brothers. She would still hide the bag on the road that led back to the Alhambra Creek parking lot, but would need to drop the bike a mile from the Briones Road entrance. That would cut ten miles off her run. It was a risk but the back roads around the park were sparsely traveled. The girl dropped the bag to the ground and fished out the gloves. No evidence could lead back to her and the gloves would prevent an errant fingerprint on the helmet or bike.

The gunshots could also attract attention even this deep into the park, she knew. After donning the gloves, she secured the helmet and after a few minutes of practice maneuvering the bike felt comfortable with its power and torque.

The motorcycle raced forward through the western region of the park. The bag was heavy and fatigue tamped down upon her, but thoughts of the bag's contents were energizing. As she came over an embankment and out of the dense foliage lining the path, she saw a full moon breaking through the clouds, reflecting silver light off the pond. She cautiously applied the brakes then stopped with a skid adjacent the barbed wire fence circling the pond. The girl kept the bike running as she fumbled with the kickstand, then dismounted, dropping the bag to the ground. She walked briskly to the edge of the fence and shot-putted the younger brother's gun into it. It plopped noisily, cracking the moon's reflection.

As the bike roared forward, the trail widened, opening into a flat field. Silver patches of moonlight scattered over the basin randomly, illuminating it with a soft glow. Near the end point of Bear Creek Trail, the girl again lighted off the Ducati and opened the gate. She quickly roared through, hearing the metal bar from the gate clank behind her. No one was in sight but a coyote's yelp echoed distantly from her left. The girl accelerated up the road leading to the park and turned right on Bear Creek Road. About three miles away, a drainage ditch terminated at the road. She had jogged the road numerous times and knew it was secluded with very few travelers even in the day. Her luck was holding—since turning onto the road, she saw no vehicles.

It was harder to see in the dark but using the odometer as a guide simplified finding the ditch. The bike roared to a stop on the right bank of the road next to the guard rail. She crossed the street and surveyed the site. Next to a mottled young oak tree, the ditch ended at the rail. This would be the marker, she thought. The girl considered putting the bag into the protruding v-crotch of the oak as she had done before, but it was too low and could be spotted from the road by a passerby. The ditch adjacent the tree was out of sight as it angled downward, providing a natural recessed opening a few feet deep. No one would see anything hidden there from the road. She buried it at that spot, smothering it with sod and leaves.

After driving a hundred yards from the bag's burial site, the girl stopped in the middle of the road and turned the bike's lights off, memorizing the landscape. Satisfied, she roared for home. As planned, the girl drove a mile before the entrance of the Pine Tree Trail. A few one-percenter homes dotted the countryside but the area was secluded. Still, the girl realized the high amplitude of the bike's engine could attract attention, so she deliberately slowed approaching the area. Even in the dim light, she recognized a guard rail she knew that protected roadsters from the ravine to its right. It would be a perfect spot to leave the bike. Banking right off the road, the girl turned the bike off and removed the helmet. For the first time, a car could be heard. She quickly walked the bike ten yards down the ravine and laid next to it while the car passed.

The girl looked at the helmet next to her and realized with a start any hair left inside could be evidence. Nothing could be left to chance. She filled the helmet with dirt and rubbed it thoroughly on the outside then secured it to the left handlebar. With a hard shove the bike picked up speed as gravity caught it. It settled with a mild thud at the ravine's floor. She listened a moment for any sounds but only the silence of the night responded.

One thing remained. The gloves were filled with dirt and after jogging three hundred yards, one was thrown into the brush. The other into a small puddle fifteen hundred yards farther along the road.

The girl looked cautiously through the ragged gingham curtains fronting the kitchen windows before opening the refrigerator and the cupboards to deposit the food. *The plan was perfect.* After depositing the food, she gathered the money in the grocery bags and fished out the black duffel bag tamped down into the biggest one. She emptied every bundle into it, realizing for the first time it was a connection to the brothers. She determined she would cut up the black bag, after cleaning it thoroughly with bleach, then at nightfall randomly scatter its remains from her car window every mile or so on the tree-lined Bear Creek Road.

Later that evening, a local TV station reported a policeman had been killed in Briones Regional Park and that two dead Hispanic men were also found on one of its hiking trails. According to the report, the police believed the killings were part of the same "drug-related incident," and had no leads as to the perpetrator of the crimes. The girl flicked her eyebrows upward knowingly and smiled.

She turned off the TV and trudged upstairs. Pain from her ribs reminded her of the previous night's happenings as she sank heavily into her computer chair. While waiting for the computer to boot, her thoughts jumped methodically from idea to idea. She would not deposit the money in the bank as she learned from a former client a deposit of ten thousand dollars or more generates an automatic currency transaction report to the IRS. No, she would be careful and restrained, depositing a few thousand randomly over the next few weeks. In a few months, the girl would move to a better place, maybe to another state. She would buy a new car, take a trip to Europe. When she returned, she would get a rescue dog. Or two. Then on to college and eventually nursing school.

The girl ran her fingers over the gun's contours as it lay on the desk. It was a link to the brothers but it was a chance she was willing to take. It would be a useful tool for another plan—the unfinished business with her mother and step-father. A Google search uncovered helpful information as to their whereabouts. Facebook more. In less than half an hour, she discovered they lived in East Palo Alto. Her step-father was working as a mechanic at a grimy auto shop nearby, her mother at a grocery store. On a whim, the girl searched for her former math professor. He was still employed at Diablo Valley College. Anger flushed the girl's cheeks. He was instantly added to the List of Unresolved Resentments. *He's probably still doing it...but not for much longer.*

The girl leaned back in her chair and sighed deeply as a tsunami of emotion overwhelmed her. For the first time since her step-father killed her dog, she wept. This time, the girl didn't suppress it. Her body convulsed as every grief, wound, and injustice bubbled forth through salted tears. It was cleansing, liberating. She knew what was coming now. For the first time, she felt empowered.

She reached for the gun and placed it carefully next to her mouse pad. She would need a plan, and as before there would be no accommodation, only justice. The second most significant moment of her life came to her like a stranger in a crowd. There was no premonition, no preamble. It intruded unexpectedly and demanded a choice—and the girl made hers.

She patted the gun lovingly like a mother would a beloved daughter's cheek before abruptly palming it with both hands. She looked down its barrel and through the sight scope as a crooked smirk filled her face.

See you soon, Stepdaddy.

THE AFTERLIFE OF ADOLF HITLER

At 3:32 P.M. on April 30th, 1945 in Berlin, Germany, Adolf Alois Hitler bit into a hydrogen cyanide capsule and shot a bullet through his brain. Upon biting into the capsule, he felt a stinging sensation course down his neck, but it was only for a millisecond as he pulled the trigger of his Walther PPK pistol into his right temple at virtually the same moment. In a panoramic burst, every moment of his life soundlessly passed before his eyes. His childhood and youth, his service in World War I, his growing political influence, his glory as *Der Fuhrer* of the German Reich. Every murder and scheme, every thought and action, no matter how mundane, he saw and comprehended before his body crumpled to the floor. Nothingness engulfed him. Blackness. Extinction.

Eternal sentience began with a ringing, followed by a peculiar ripping sound. Then, consciousness. Still dressed in his military uniform, hovering at the top of the ceiling, he looked down at himself. *I'm...alive?!* He saw blood course from his temple before it stanched. It was odd looking at one's self in three dimensions. He had seen himself in countless cinematic reels and in the mirror, but this was different. *I want to get a closer look.* The thought somehow served as a command as he instantly floated down next to his body before crouching to his haunches. He reached out toward his military hat that had fallen askew next to his body but couldn't feel anything. He tried again and again but it was like trying to grab air. *How can I be alive yet...dead?*

"Adi, what's happening to us?!"

Standing next to him was Eva Braun, his bride, dressed in the same clothes she was wearing when she joined him in suicide. He stood up and looked at her. Fear and confusion contorted her face.

"Eva?"

"What's happening?" she asked, almost hysterical.

Confusion almost overwhelmed him. "I think we're...dead," he said, deliberately.

She tried holding his arm for comfort but there was nothing to grasp. Any momentary control dissipated. "Why can't I touch you?!"

Hitler tried comforting her by exuding a commanding tone, but he was as confused as she. He had always believed when one died it meant eternal nothingness—a ceasing of being. Yes, he gave lip service to religious superstition when he told the gullible German people that Divine Providence had led him to his work of re-establishing the German empire after its defeat in World War I and the humiliation of the Treaty of Versailles. But he never believed it. While he hated Communism, he agreed with Karl Marx that religion was the opiate of the masses. And he had used the reflexive respect for the numinous to gain power.

Eva grew increasingly hysterical. "What do we do now, Adi?! What do we do?!"

He despised such uncontrolled expressions of emotion

in life and wouldn't tolerate it in death. *I'm leaving this room.* He effortlessly moved toward the *Führerbunker* door but stopped short when he heard its characteristic metallic creaking. Before he could move, his personal adjutant, Otto Gunsche, entered the room along with his physician, Werner Haase.

Gunsche's hand instinctively covered his mouth as he watched Haase kneel next to the bodies. He checked the pulse in Hitler's neck, then Eva's.

"He's dead," said Haase.

"I'm right here!"

"We follow his last wishes—we douse them with petro and burn them," said Gunsche.

Hitler and Eva screamed and yelled at them but to no avail. They were invisible and non-corporeal. They watched his valet, Heinz Linge, and numerous soldiers come in and wrap their corpses in gray blankets and solemnly carry them out. Hitler and Eva attempted to walk out with them but one of the soldiers dutifully closed the bunker door with a clang, causing them to stop short. They grasped desperately at the door handle, again and again.

"Just walk through the door, *mein Fuhrer*," said a voice behind them. They snapped their heads backward toward the sound. It was a man dressed in a Nazi military uniform with a round face and short, cropped hair. The scars on his nose and chin were gone as was the unique indentation on his left cheek, but Hitler knew him instantly.

"Ernst Rohm?"

"I'm sure you thought you'd never see me again."

Hitler long ago quashed any guilt regarding the murder of his former friend. Rohm had once been Hitler's most trusted confidant and ally, wielding great power that some said was second only to *Der Fuhrer* himself. He had been an early member of the Nazi Party and co-founded and commanded the Storm Battalion, which had ever served as the cat's paw in the Nazis' lust for power. After Hitler assumed complete control of the German government in 1934, he, and other Nazi elites, came to fear the Storm Battalion and Rohm's influence. Along with other rivals, Hitler ordered his assassination during the Night of the Long Knives purge.

"I've been watching you since my death. I was your friend, your comrade. We could've done great things together."

"I don't want to hear from you," sneered Hitler, looking away.

"Not that any of it matters now," said Rohm wistfully. Eva watched him intently as he floated just off the floor.

"Did he tell you what he did to me, my dear?" asked Rohm. "He had me murdered. He thought I was his rival but I wasn't. I was his friend."

"Adi?" importuned Eva.

He averted her gaze. "That's in the past," Hitler said with an imperious wave of his hand.

"What year is it?" asked Rohm. The question caught them off guard.

"It's April 30th, 1945," said Eva.

"Almost eleven years have passed since my death! I can't believe it," said Rohm. "It seems like just a few moments ago. You'll find a lot of things different in this place."

Eva studied him carefully. "Like what?" she asked.

"You can fly. Walk through walls. And know the thoughts of all the dead around you."

Hitler folded his arms. "Continue," he commanded.

"We are in the spirit world now. These are our spirit bodies."

For the first time, Hitler scanned his spirit body. He felt neither hot nor cold and was perfectly comfortable. Movement, too, was easy and natural. Eva actually giggled as she put her hand through the door.

"This is kind of fun!"

"This is not a time for joviality!" thundered Hitler.

But this new dimension was jarring, even to him. This was a domain unbound and unencumbered by the laws of the temporal world he was accustomed to.

"You'll find the concept of time passing very foreign and difficult to comprehend in this disembodied state," offered Rohm, reading Eva's thoughts.

"You can read my thoughts?" asked Eva.

"See them. Know them. Whatever anyone thinks here, however fleetingly or unwillingly, is instantly visible to all around them," Rohm said.

He was right. For the first time Hitler noticed images appear haphazardly in the space above them. He intuitively knew the thoughts of Eva and Rohm as quickly as they thought them. He could clearly see the wounded contempt Rohm held for him, the devotion of Eva. With sudden panic, Hitler wondered what it was going to be like where his most private thoughts were open to all—where there could be no clever trick of language to seduce, no disguising of intent, no seeming, only being.

"Indeed," said Rohm, smirking.

The disdain Hitler held for those around him, even those loyal to him, was evident in his thoughts and person. Eva looked at his visualized thoughts and then at him with a combination of fear and disappointment.

"Eva, you knew what I was," Hitler said quietly.

"You need to see what happens to your body. Follow me," interrupted Rohm.

In a moment he ascended through the ceiling. The *Führerbunker* was beneath the Chancellery with concrete walls four feet thick. They hesitated a moment but floated upward and were instantly outside hovering over the Reich Chancellery.

"I think I'm going to like this!" said the ever-cheerful Eva.

From his vantage point above the Reich Chancellery, Hitler could see the devastation of Berlin. Building after building as far as he could see had been destroyed or damaged. Sounds of troops shouting and bullets riddled the air. He wished he could go higher and in an instant he was. He could now clearly see the Brandenburg Gate and Russian incursions forming on the west of the Konigsplatz near the Reichstag.

"Over here," shouted Rohm.

Rohm was standing near a newly-dug pit that was just outside the bunker. A handful of soldiers were dousing something in the pit with gasoline. Quick as thought, Hitler and Eva stood next to Rohm.

"That's you," said Rohm, pointing toward the bodies in the pit. Hitler's and Eva's bodies were covered with gray woolen blankets, but Hitler could clearly make out his left hand. He brought his spirit left hand up to look at it, as if somehow it was connected to the one dangling in the dirt beneath him. His beloved dog Blondi, too, lay next to his corpse. They watched as one of the soldiers struck a match and threw it into the pit. Fire immediately flamed over the remains. The soldiers solemnly watched for a moment and in unison silently struck the Nazi salute.

"I don't want to watch this anymore," said Eva.

Rohm pointed toward the soldiers. "Look at the living men."

"There's a sheath of light around each of them," said Hitler, noticing it for the first time.

"What is it?" Asked Eva.

"Those who are alive with bodies have a sheath of light or aura that somehow protects them from us."

"Why would they need protection from us?" asked Hitler. "We can't touch anything or anyone."

"It protects them from being possessed by us."

"That doesn't make sense," sneered Hitler.

"Those who are addicted to tobacco, alcohol, sex, food, and other things will have that sheath peel away when they're compromised—such as when they fall unconscious drunk or in sleep. It starts from the head and peels downward. When that happens, we disembodied can 'jump' into them with our spirit bodies and feel physical pleasure again. That's the only way to get physical satisfactions for us disembodied," explained Rohm.

"So, if you're addicted to something and you die, you're permanently cut off from it?" asked Hitler.

"Yes," said Rohm. "When you die, your physical appetites and addictions go with it to the grave."

"I don't understand," said Eva.

"You will. Give it time. That's all we have now."

The fire in the pit blazed a while longer, its flames coloring the soldiers' faces orange and red. It was strange watching one's own body burn in front of you, Hitler thought. Yet he felt compelled to watch it somehow. For the first time he felt fear in his newfound state.

"This is all so peculiar," Hitler said.

"I know, my friend."

"Where are we exactly?" asked Eva.

Rohm folded his spirit arms across his chest. "I've talked to other dead about this. Some say it's the spirit world. Others call it limbo. Some say it's Hell itself."

"Maybe a combination of all three," mused Hitler.

"I never thought there was life after death, and I know you didn't either, Adi. But here we are," said Rohm.

A steel door creaked open behind them, drawing their attention. Hitler's propaganda minister, Joseph Goebbels, and his wife, Magda, somberly walked out the bunker door and up its steps. They were followed by three soldiers carrying gasoline cans and gray blankets.

"Wait here," they heard Goebbels order.

They watched as Goebbels and his wife trudged around the bunker out of sight of the soldiers, then kiss and hug each other in solemn finality.

"She killed all her children," said Rohm grimly.

"Magda killed the children?" asked Eva. Rohm solemnly nodded his head.

Magda walked a few paces away from Goebbels. They looked longingly at each other, tears staining their faces. Goebbels drew a pistol from his holster and shot her in the head, then himself. Eva gasped.

"Watch," said Rohm.

Almost immediately the spirits of the Goebbels ascended from their now dead bodies and hovered above them. They watched as the Goebbels reacted with the same bewilderment and fear. It was all too familiar. They loomed no more than twenty feet away, yet the newly departed were oblivious to their presence.

"We should help them," said Eva.

"Give them a moment," said Rohm.

"Why can't they see or hear us?" Hitler asked.

Rohm hesitated before answering. "Here, you see what you want to see when you're ready to see it."

"How do you know she killed the children?" asked Eva.

"It's a knowing."

"I don't understand," said Hitler, annoyed.

"Waves of knowledge will come unbidden to you, as you'll soon see. That revelatory touch once told me we are in a pool of infinite intelligence," offered Rohm.

Hitler and Eva both nodded, not fully comprehending.

"There are really no secrets on this side of the veil of life," continued Rohm.

This was not the Ernst Rohm Hitler knew in mortality. This man was subdued, humble—gentle, even.

"Death changes you," said Rohm, reading his thoughts.

Upon hearing the second shot, the soldiers came around the corner of the bunker and wrapped the Goebbels' bodies in blankets and carried them to the pit adjacent the one holding the still-smoldering remains of Hitler and Braun. Their bodies, too, were doused with gasoline and lit on fire. Goebbels and his wife watched, transfixed upon the inferno in front of them.

"Joseph! Magda!" yelled Hitler.

"*Mein Fuhrer*?" said Magda. "Is that really you?"

"Yes, my dear."

More dead Nazi faithful soon found their way to Hitler. Before long, they numbered in the hundreds of thousands. Rohm, along with Reinhard Heydrich, became Hitler's closest confidants to the envy of the other Nazi aristocrats.

Heydrich had been a personal favorite of Hitler's in life, calling him "irreplaceable" upon his death and "the man with the iron will." After a severe chastisement due to Heydrich's preventable death from an insurgent's attack in Prague, they happily reconciled.

Plans were soon discussed among the Nazi elite as how to dominate within this new realm, but infighting grew as rivals in life had remained so in death. Some openly blamed Hitler for losing the war, most notably Himmler and Goring. Hitler was uncomfortable with the additions of Himmler and Goring and everyone knew it with his thoughts of malice ever unmasking him. He had not forgotten how Himmler had tried to make an unauthorized, backroom deal with the Americans at the war's end, or how Goring had sent him a telegram asking that he be allowed to become leader of Germany as Hitler was cut off in the bunker.

Their thoughts toward him were equally hostile. The absence of physicality birthed candor and audacity, allowing anyone to say or think what they wanted without fear of reprisal. Hitler was surprised at the animosity so many held against him. Still, there was solace and an unspoken consolation in consorting with others as loathsome as one's self.

The loss of the war still stung Hitler. In his arrogance, he had been sure of victory. He grudgingly admitted to his fellow Nazis that it was a tactical error to attack the Russians. That decision was the hinge upon which the war turned, he realized to his great regret, as it created a war on two fronts and united the Allies.

The undisciplined nature of his Nazi companions gradually dissolved the initial bond that brought them together. Some due to disenchantment with him, others because of discontent with the spirit world. All sought comfort in things physical and earthly, though the pleasure of food, drink, and sex were not as easily obtained. All left seeking what satisfaction they could glean in a strange, new underworld. Even Heydrich and Eva eventually left him.

The loss of Eva's companionship was the most poignant. Not since the suicide of his niece, Geli Raubal, had he felt such a wound. Still, he steeled himself to disappointment in death as he had in life. He would adapt to this realm and conquer it the way he had Germany. The first step, he determined, was to acclimate to this dimension. And then to find new followers.

The unnecessity of sleep troubled Hitler the most in his new sphere of existence. In sleep, one could escape the cares and stresses of the world. But not here as the need for sleep died with the body. Yet he also realized it was an opportunity. There were other intriguing attributes of this dimension—the ability to fly. He would fly into the clouds and scale the earth from the stratosphere. Once, on a whim, he thought about flying to the moon but upon entering the earth's mesosphere, an invisible barrier stopped him.

Europe was his first choice. He would set down wherever curiosity struck and observe. In the bigger cities, the dead were especially fascinating. Those with tobacco and alcohol addictions were ever in misery. They would hover over the living who would smoke and imbibe with the mortals, utterly oblivious to the drama unfolding about them. Those dead who yearned for tobacco would curse in frustration as they clutched at the cigarettes or cigars held by the mortals, while the alcohol-addicted would wait in pubs for the characteristic light peel of a drunken physical soul. Then, numerous spirits around them would hurtle themselves toward the opening to experience the temporary satisfaction of alcohol bliss. *Spirits seeking the bliss of spirits*, he mused to himself after witnessing possession for the first time.

Beer halls were not only a meeting place for the living but for the dead. While a teetotaler in life, he frequented such establishments for sociality. Even in this disembodied realm he was still famous, and never turned down an opportunity to regale others with stories of his dark deeds and glory. He enjoyed the festive nature of those as dispossessed as him as it helped to relieve the insufferable boredom that pervaded the spirits of all the disembodied.

Other places in the spirit world were not as pleasant. Not long after his fellow Nazis left him, he came upon a massive field where tens of thousands of dead were fighting. The dead comprised some from his time but there were many from other time periods. He was not unacquainted with war, but this was a war of another sort—a war of words and thoughts. He could plainly see and hear the violent thoughts they hurled toward one another—thoughts of enmity as pronounced as his. Notwithstanding the futility of physical confrontation, everyone in the field was attempting to assault their enemy. A kick or a blow that would've killed a man in life left him as before. Others would feverishly pantomime lurid sexual perversions upon their enemies but to no conclusion. One thing was certain: these were the most miserable souls he had come across in his short sojourn in the netherworld.

As he watched the misery about him, a few German soldiers approached. For a few moments, hostilities ceased as Hitler attempted to rouse those dead to join his cause, but they laughed him to scorn. Hitler felt comfortable among these damned, but humiliated, flew off until he found a place without any dead or living. The sun was setting in the physical world and with it, night.

No sooner had he sat down on a large boulder when he sensed something. A feeling unlike anything he had ever encountered. It was as if an invisible cloud of evil and malice engulfed him. He somehow knew it was the harbinger of a presence. Hitler stood up and looked toward an empty field to his left where the feeling-cloud emanated when he saw someone walking toward him through the underbrush. It was a man. The man wore a thin black robe that went down to his ankles. Wrapped around his waist was an ornamental cloth napkin. As the personage strode closer, suffocating fear gripped him. *Why am I afraid of this man?* As the man approached, the cloud of pure evil and malice grew stronger, more palpable, yet it was now coupled with what he perceived were barely-contained anger and resentment. He sensed something else too: this man possessed great cunning and knowledge.

In a realm where one cannot hide what they truly are, Hitler then knew who approached. It was the Devil himself. *It can't be.*

"It is," came the spoken reply from the man in the black robe.

He stopped short only a few feet from Hitler. He appeared so unlike the preconceived fantasies mortals believed, Hitler thought. There were no horns or tail, no serpentine forked tongue; this was not a bipedal man-dragon with wings breathing fire. It was a man. A man about Hitler's height with blonde hair cut in a Prince Valiant style. He was clean-shaven, handsome, and looked to be in his early thirties. He was utterly normal-looking except for his eyes. His sclera was white but the irises were black, exuding malice and contempt that starkly contrasted with his otherwise becoming features.

"I'm Lucifer. Welcome to the netherworld," he said, bowing slightly in salutation.

"What is that?" Hitler blurted, pointing to the apron. The Prince of Devils cocked his head and smirked as if amused by the question.

"It is an emblem of my power and priesthoods," he said in perfect German.

"Who are you, really?"

"You know," he said, the smirk growing wider.

"You're Satan? Lucifer?" Hitler asked, still not believing.

A becoming smile crossed his face. "Yes, those are two of my names."

"What do you want with me?"

"I want you to help me in my work," he said matter-of-factly, raising his voice slightly. The prospect of subservience to one who had long enjoyed the mantle of power was instantly unappealing to the former *Fuhrer* of the Third Reich.

"I know you've thought about how you can dominate and rule in this realm, but I wouldn't try that if I were you."

Hitler was taken aback that the Devil knew those thoughts as he was not in his presence when he thought them.

The Devil smirked. "Oh yes, I know your thoughts," he said contemptuously.

Hitler feared him but began feeling more comfortable and even a strange kinship with the man.

"All the liars, murderers, adulterers, thieves, hypocrites, whores, sorcerers, criminals and other infidels, inhabit this kingdom. *My* kingdom," he said most deliberately.

The veneer of courtesan chivalry the Devil exuded was now gone. "*I* am the Prince of Hell, not you. *I* rule here, not you."

"And how would you stop me?" asked Hitler defiantly.

In a moment Hitler felt an oppressive, unseen cloud of power upon him. It was debilitating and anguishing, its chief characteristic a palpable, coercive compulsion beating down upon him. He had never felt anything like it.

"What you are experiencing is the iron yoke, the chains, the shackles of Hell. Always remember this: YOU...ARE...MINE," he sneered.

Hitler dropped to his knees in pain, humiliation filling him. "I'll never join you."

"You did in your mortal life although you didn't know it," he said as he sat down on the large boulder Hitler had vacated. "Think carefully now before you respond. Help me in my work willingly and there will be a place for you."

"No. NO," glared Hitler.

Lucifer looked at him an uncomfortably long time, hate filling his face. "So be it."

And in an instant, the Devil and the pain were gone. Humiliated, he let out a loud yawp in frustration and anger.

After the encounter, he wandered the world for years, or so it seemed to him. He watched Germany re-build after the war. He expected some monument or relic of his contributions, but found none. His pride was dashed when he sat in on a lecture at a German university and heard the contempt of the crowd for him and his political philosophies. Most painful of all was the rejection of Nazism. He realized with finality that national socialism was an utter failure. It was even worse than the humiliation of the Treaty of Versailles. There was no disputing it— everything he worked for was repudiated.

Friendless and rejected, he traveled to America. If nothing else, it would, he hoped, lighten the oppressive lethargy he suffered. For Hitler, the most difficult element of the non-physical realm called death was not the absence of physical satisfaction but the insufferable boredom. There was no escape in sleep, no physical pleasures to enjoy. Just lethargy.

Upon arriving in New York, he looked forward to learning English, hoping it would dispel the unending ennui. He came upon the idea that the best place to learn would be with children in kindergarten classes. And so, unseen to New York City's innocents, the former *Fuhrer* of the Third Reich sat in on their classes and learned their language.

Learning was so much easier in the underworld. While a physical being, learning required repetition and practice. Even those with intellectual talent had their limitations, but not here. In the spirit dimension, learning came instantaneously. He quickly established a routine of listening to deepen his understanding of the language, reading snippets of newspapers left askew in parks or pubs, and engaging in occasional conversations with other spirit passersby. He came to enjoy some of these exchanges, but not all. He was constantly set upon by dead Allied soldiers trying to fight him but he never engaged, as physical violence in the realm of shadow and damnation was simply not possible.

More unsettling than the constant reminders of his state was night. While he had no physical addictions to contend with as so many in this dimension, the boredom and oppressive languor upon his soul was somehow amplified in darkness.

The lack of privacy was also troubling. The innumerable hordes of the disembodied was always surprising, their numbers easily surpassing the living. After traveling throughout America and Canada, he flew to the far reaches of the world in hopes of privacy but was ever-disappointed. There were some moments of solitude. He was delighted to find the Andes rarely frequented by the dead. Antarctica, too. He would sit atop one of its many mountains alone and think of what could have been. The deep forests of northern Canada and a few uninhabited Pacific islands were also favorites. Cemeteries, too, ironically, were clear of the dead.

Eventually he decided to go back to Europe and toured every European country, including Russia. He was always enchanted by France and settled there for a time, learning French the way he did English. After the humiliating university lecture incident in Germany, he avoided Austria and Germany at first, yet in time longed for them.

The changes to Austria and Germany surprised him. Any vestige of the war was now gone. There were no bombed-out buildings or streets filled with debris. The face of Berlin had changed, too. Numerous glass-encased buildings towered over the city, as well as other buildings of an architecture style foreign to him. It was a bustling city filled with commerce and activity. The staid black automobiles of his time were replaced with those of various innovative styles and colors. Fashion styles had changed, too, especially among the youth. Women were wearing pants and shorts. In his time, such displays would have been disgraceful. He had seen such styles in America and Canada but assumed it would not happen in his beloved Germany. The absence of military personnel was also striking; there were no men in uniforms to be seen. He was grateful that he still was clothed in the military uniform he wore when he died. It was the last vestige of his former life and was one of the few satisfactions he now possessed.

Nostalgia persuaded him to visit the *Führerbunker*. To his surprise, a parking lot adjacent to large apartment complexes had paved over where he spent his final days as a mortal. Perhaps he was in the wrong place, he thought, so he flew high in the air to get his bearings. There was the Brandenburg Gate to the northeast, the Berliner Dome far to the east, and the Victory Column to the west. But something south of the Brandenburg Gate caught his attention. He saw numerous rectangular gray blocks of stones resembling massive boxes arranged neatly, one after the other. Curious, he flew down to inspect them. To his right he saw a sign, "Memorial to the Murdered Jews of Europe." *A memorial to Jews, but none to me?* To his right he watched in horror as a group of Hassidic Jews silently strode through the walkways of the nondescript monument. This was not his Berlin. A fresh wave of futility and self-pity coursed through him as he sat atop one of the monoliths watching the people. He watched a gust of wind blow through the mortals, causing some to lose their balance and others their hats. How he wished he could feel the wind blow about him and feel the warmth of the sun on his face. He never believed he'd miss such seemingly simple things.

He needed to know how much time had passed. After meandering through the city, he saw a middle-aged woman reading a newspaper while she smoked a cigarette and sipped on coffee in an outdoor café.

"She's mine! SHE'S MINE!" the spirit yelled at him as he approached.

"I just want to see the date on the paper."

He flew around to catch the date: Saturday, August 25th, 2029. *I've been dead 84 years?*

Something drew his attention to the east. A brilliant glory filled the sky from horizon to horizon. For a moment he thought it was the sun itself intruding upon the earth's atmosphere. Screams of terror could be heard while some stood and watched solemnly. Others sunk to their knees and prayed. As the glory of the light penetrated the ground, every building caught fire and the very earth itself set aflame.

Hitler heard the clearing of a trumpet sound loud and long. The instant it ceased, he found himself in a black void, floating in space. He saw the faint light of stars and sensed he was infinitely far from Earth. Awful shrieks and screams reverberated through the space about him, jarring him with an unnatural, harrowing fear. In an instant he was moving at an incalculable speed, and then, just as suddenly, was motionless. Almost immediately he sensed something was coming for him. Something awful. Something beyond horror. And so it was. It came upon him quietly, yet fearfully, like a whisper from a monster behind a door in the bitter watches of an endless night. Thick darkness billowed toward, then around, and through him. The blackness consumed him and with it came shattering pain beyond the ken of mortal imagination. It was as if every atom of his being was bathed in fire. *The pain of damnation,* a voice within his mind said.

Another dimension of the torture was the simultaneous crush of an indescribable bitterness. When he had first arrived in the benighted realm of shadow, he could see the light of some stars but now he could see nothing. He could actually feel the vapor of the inky blackness upon his spirit body, which only added to his terror. *Outer darkness,* said the unbidden voice.

Emotional pain as penetrating as the soul-borne torture descended upon him, adding a new dimension to his misery. It was despair beyond mortal understanding added to crushing loneliness and all-consuming fear. The loneliness, too, was overwhelming with thought his only companion. Out of the void, a thought pressed itself upon his mind more forcefully than any of the previous revelations: *You will be judged.* The thought of somehow coming into the presence of a divine being instantly racked his soul with inexpressible terror.

Time went by—or so he believed. Was it a year since the torture started? Five? A hundred? Or was it only minutes? Since his mortal death, he'd lost all sense of time, but in perdition's flame the sense of time's continuity was even more diminished. Whether an experience took a second or a year was incomprehensible. It was a realm where rules of time, space, and mass were simply inapplicable. Sadness and grief beyond measure now overwhelmed him. *Second Death.* He wished in the innermost parts of his heart that he could cease to exist...but it was not to be. A new revelatory wave of intelligence came upon him, telling him he was an eternal being and that his soul could never be destroyed. He intuitively knew it was true and it only added to his anguish. The thought that perhaps this *was* his end, that he would suffer so, alone in outer darkness—forever—filled him with indescribable dread. This suffering was enormity multiplied by infinity. The sheer combination of such weighted emotional and physical suffering was a descent below all things; the depth, breadth, width, and height of such misery was unknowable; how sore, how exquisite, how hard to bear such torture was unfathomable to mortals and even the gods themselves. He again instinctively knew that only those justly consigned to such suffering can comprehend what is endured. A new revelation pressed itself upon his mind: *eternal punishment*; *everlasting punishment.*

Soon thereafter, another damnable impression came to him: more suffering was yet to come. He screamed and wailed in abject grief and terror with the premonition. *Someone help me! Mercy!* An unexpected answer immediately came with more force and emphasis than any of the previous revelations: throughout all the infinite worlds, there had never been such universal devastation and misery caused by just one man. He was responsible for the killing of 25,301,132 million people, among them 6,011,235 Jews; an additional 28,703,459 soldiers died due to the war in the European Theater of World War II, and 30,753,929 more souls suffered as a result of his actions.

As soon as the voice passed, in the void before him, a three-dimensional panorama of a seemingly innumerable number of people paraded before him. At first, the illumination from the spectacle was welcome in the hellish pitch. Until then his basic senses were exempt from the suffering endured. But no more. Somehow, in the spatial rift before him he saw and felt the torture and misery each soul endured at his hand. Each violence, each crime upon every man, woman, and child he viewed and felt with a perfect synesthetic clarity. He heard the shrieks of each soul affected, smelled the rotting flesh of bodies piled into train cars, felt the grief of the bullied, tasted the hunger and thirst of the starved, endured the broken heart of a mother ripped from her child, understood the horror of loss, breathed the fear of torture, choked in unjust powerlessness, drowned in injustice's flame. Soul by soul, scene by scene, he suffered what his victims experienced; a coloratura of infinite suffering. Grief, despair, pain, loneliness and agony to the uttermost farthing, beyond mortal comprehension, were now infused upon the being known as Adolf Hitler. He had become death; he was now a vessel of wrath, of everlasting misery. Eventually he resigned himself to his fate. And with that resignation, any remnant of hope fled. The torment continued for what he perceived as an eternity. And so it was.

And in a moment, it was gone.

The relentless cascading menagerie of his victims' suffering was his no more. The unending scenes of horror also ceased. He scanned his being—there was no more pain. A new revelation came to him: every sin of thought and deed, no matter how trivial, had been accounted for and paid in full. It was strange now, even foreign, to not be racked with infinite torture. *What now?*

In a twinkling, even before the thought finished coursing through his mind, he found himself in front of a building. After an eternity within the very vortex of perdition's flame, he collapsed to his knees and in a start, realized he had a body again. It was unnatural after such a long absence. As was the light. It took a few moments to gather himself; he flexed and unflexed his hands and ran them over his body and head. He noticed another change— he no longer wore a military uniform. He was now dressed in a cream-colored silken robe and sandals.

A voice disturbed him.

"Adolf Alois Hitler."

He looked up toward the voice to gaze upon the most magnificent being he had ever seen. The man was dressed in a white robe that glowed light. Around his person a becoming light glittered and gently pulsed. In his right hand was a golden shepherd's staff. The man watched him intently.

"Who are you?" Hitler asked, struggling to stand up.

"What you would call an angel. I have been commanded to escort you to the bar where you will be judged for your deeds done in the flesh." An involuntary gasp escaped Hitler's lips.

"Where are your wings?"

"A common mistake."

The angel stood in front of a massive staircase leading to a building that vaguely reminded Hitler of the Parthenon in ancient Athens. Towering Doric columns introduced the building's entrance and portico while walkways of becoming white limestone and arched colonnades extended outward. His neck craned to take in the architectural marvel. Three towers atop the great edifice extended heavenward with golden spires piercing the cloudless blue sky above. It was the most breathtaking building he had ever seen.

"This is the Hall of Judgment," Hitler said aloud, somehow knowing.

"Yes."

In the building next to it, he could see through the hall's colonnade to a water fountain commanding the ground. Around its pink travertine circular walkway was a garden with carefully arranged shrubbery and flowers of every type. Some of the flowers emitted a glistening rainbow of colors that extended outward. Others emitted sounds. Others both. As far as he could see, dazzling gardens and walkways weaved in and among the city's buildings. Off in the distance, he heard dogs barking, horses neighing, birds fluting, music playing. *This is a glorious place to behold.* Hitler allowed himself a smile.

The building where he materialized, he guessed, was in an administrative district, and like those around it, glowed with light. Men and women in small groups were talking, peopling the gardens. Some were striding purposefully on some business, and all were dressed in dazzling white robes. As some strolled in the walkways nearby, he saw soundless bursts of concentered, white light form around them as they disappeared. In the piazza across from him, he watched while oblong-shaped wormholes of light formed in empty space and in an instant a man or woman appeared.

"Inter-dimensional travel," the angel offered, reading

his mind.

"Is this Heaven?"

"No. It's time," the angel said waving his right arm with a detectable tinge of impatience.

As they walked up the steps and through the portico, the massive golden doors swung open to greet them. Entering the atrium, Hitler gasped. The interior was imposing, vast. His eyes were immediately drawn to the coffered ceiling above, where gold leaf and precious jewels adorned sunken octagonal panels. As with the outside of the building, the ornamental plaster of the walls was aglow with a soft luminescence. Clerestory windows outlined and trimmed by pearls, emeralds, and sapphires bedazzled the interior while crepuscular rays of light fell through the windows, lighting the interior in evenly spaced columns.

"Is this a church?"

"No. And yes," said the angel.

The interior resembled an artful fusion of Gothic, Renaissance, and Romanesque architecture that was at once dazzling yet comely. A colonnade of Ionic columns lined the nave with pews filled with people wearing cream-colored robes like his. Hitler and the angel passed an Ionic column parallel the narthex and entered the nave. At the front of the hall, behind the chancel, was raised Amphitheatre seating that extended almost to the ceiling. It, too, was filled with people. Above the raised bema were three immense, cloistered apses adorned with an assortment of carvings accentuated by an exquisite amalgam of gems that defied language. The colonnades lining the nave also exhibited engravings of astonishing craftsmanship. At the front of the hall, the elevated chancel extended horizontally in both directions toward arched entryways, accentuated by a balustrade of shimmering ivory. In the center of the chancel, a golden, crescent-shaped bema extended slightly outward. Almost directly below the bema, at the center of the room, stood a raised platform with a mahogany, circular bar. *The Bar of Judgment.* To the right bordering the wall was another witness stand, to the left another.

As they passed into the nave, in unison, all souls in the hall turned toward them. No one spoke. All seemed to be waiting in earnest solemnity for something. Hitler felt a shock ripple through him: To his right, seated together were the most prominent members of the Nazi Party and its leaders.

And Eva.

She crinkled her mouth into a forced smile mingled with sadness. He caught the gaze of his old friends, Speer, Rohm, Himmel and others who bowed their heads slightly downward in grave salutation. Their appearance was different somehow. They all looked youthful, beautiful even.

The angel leaned to him and whispered, "They were all judged and resurrected eons ago while you languished in outer darkness. The bodies they now possess befit their former wickedness. They are Telestial beings." Hitler nodded politely, not fully understanding.

All eyes were fixed on him as the angel led him up the nave's aisle. Finally, they arrived at the bar.

"Stand there, please," commanded the angel, pointing to the raised stand.

Hitler obediently stepped onto the solitary stair and upon entering, grabbed the wooden bar before him with both hands. The angel took a few steps forward and faced the assembly, a solemn sentinel.

Almost immediately there was a commotion to the left of the chancel that caught Hitler's attention. Hushed voices could be heard as four beings entered the hall. They were even more glorious than the angel who accompanied him. Two walked toward the end of the chancel to Hitler's right and took positions flanking the entrance-way. The other two did the same, ensconcing themselves near the left entrance.

"All stand, please," said the angel who accompanied Hitler.

All eyes in unison fixed to the left entrance-way of the chancel as a hushed, solemn silence settled upon the great hall. All watched enrapt as blazing white light brighter than a million suns filled the chancel and streamed into the hall. The glory increased as if it proceeded something. It did.

Him.

A man whose brightness and glory defied all mortal description. As he silently walked toward the bema at the center of the chancel, golden-white light continued to swirl and stream around him, filling the hall. But there was something else. Even more enthralling than the glory accompanying this being was the love that emanated from him. A perfect, unconditional love that defied comprehension. It flowed from him like an unquenchable fire even more than the glory accompanying his person.

Coupled with the all-encompassing glory and love emanating from the man was also an aura of astonishing authority. Hitler instinctively knew other things about him, too: he was omnipotent and omniscient. And perfect.

But it was the love that defined him. Hitler had never felt such emotions, nor thought such love could exist. It was love and compassion beyond mortal imagination, filling the deepest recesses of his heart.

As the man arrived at the bema, the glory swirling and emanating about his person dissipated to a surrounding glow. For the first time, Hitler could now see him plainly. He appeared to be in his early thirties, around six feet tall and weighed approximately one hundred and seventy-five pounds. He had a mesomorphic body type and was masculine in manner and mien. Dark auburn hair combed back and parted down the middle of his head fell gracefully around his neck and ears, obscuring them except for his ear lobes. He wore a neatly trimmed beard that was slightly parted as it extended past his chin, its coloring matching his hair. His ruddy countenance accentuated piercing grey-blue eyes that rested their gaze naturally upon that about him. His attire, too, was glorious to behold. The silken robe he wore terminated above his wrists and extended down to his sandaled feet. It glowed with a brilliant golden luster as if each nanometer of its fabric were made of diamonds. The sheen and glory of the robe reminded Hitler of the gleam from sunlight bouncing off untouched mountain snow.

"Everyone be seated," the angel commanded.

The sound of rustling silk pervaded the hall as all obeyed. Hitler unconsciously turned his head to his right where he saw a number of men filled the first row, their faces contorted with disdain. He knew their identities instantly, yet that damnable voice came again: *The leaders of the failed July 20th plot.* An uncomfortable beat passed between them before he gladly turned away.

The man at the bema looked at him with a pursed smile and almost instantly Hitler began to tremble uncontrollably.

"What have you done with your mortal life?" the man finally asked him in a quiet voice.

Immediately upon the question, the same three-dimensional, holographic panorama Hitler had seen upon his death and in outer darkness projected in the air near the luminescent wall to his right. Every deed, thought, and action, no matter how mundane or trivial, was displayed. There was no denying—or hiding—anything. One couldn't. It was simply impossible, as every deed in mortality was shown, along with its accompanying thoughts and intentions.

The most glorious of men settled before the bema, quietly watching the panorama before him. Every thought, lie, deceit, and murder; every wickedness was there along with the accompanying thoughts. Embarrassment beyond expression filled Hitler's soul. What compounded the shame was he now somehow possessed a perfect recollection of all his guilt. To have every ungodly act exposed in front of so many was infinitely mortifying. Some audibly gasped. Those who were once his friends saw his thoughts of contempt as he manipulated them to his dark will. He could feel their eyes upon him and for a moment, wished he were back in perdition's flame. The thought sent a chill through him.

The man at the bar looked expectantly at Hitler. He scanned his life, looking for anything to show him that was good or praiseworthy.

"I won the Iron Cross Second Class medal in World War I for bravery. Also, the Black Wound Badge," he said in a breaking voice while pointing toward the scenes in the panorama. "I saved many of my comrades' lives."

"That glorified you," the man said in perfect kindness. And he was right. Above the deeds were Hitler's thoughts of vanity and the desire to impress.

"You did show great courage—that is true—but the motives were not equal to the deeds."

Hitler was surprised that the scenes that gave him the most pleasure, even peace, were those from his troubled childhood. He saw with longing his boyhood home in Linz, Austria, watched himself painting and drawing in his room to escape his father, viewed himself happily playing with his childhood friends, delighted again in the excitement of a first kiss shared, observed his mother kissing him on the forehead at the dinner table. In a start he wondered if his mother was in the crowd.

"Your mother is behind you to your left," the man at the bar said gently.

Hitler twisted his neck backward to the left and saw his mother sitting in the front row, tears coursing down her face. In a burst of emotion, he realized how much he loved her. He wanted to run to her, hold her, tell her how much he missed her, how much she meant to him, but an unseen power held him in place.

He turned back toward the panorama and saw himself receive news of his mother's death. He realized that was the moment something changed in him. He saw his anger and misanthropy growing, relived again his rejections from art school, his subsequent poverty in Vienna, his growing anti-Semitism, his time in the German army during World War I, his ascent to power, the adulation of the German people, the loss of the war, his suicide and sojourn in the spirit world. And then, most chillingly, his eternity in outer darkness.

"It's time to hear from the witnesses," said the man at the bar.

Hitler now knew why there were so many filling the hall. Victim after victim, came forth and entered the witness stands to confirm their personal experience as shown in the unending panoramic vista of murder and horror. Most poignant were the Jewish victims who were brought before the tribunal. As untold numbers recounted their suffering, Hitler once again could feel the emotions his victims experienced when they were murdered or starved or hung or shot, just as he had before in the abyss. But this time it was different. He now somehow felt all the suffering the Jews experienced at his hand from the beginning of the Holocaust to the end of their lives. To experience this was soul-wrenching, but coupled with the shame of viewing so many scenes of dehumanizing brutality in front of he who was all-holy was unendurable. Hitler wished he could call down mountains upon himself to hide from the man at the bar but knew it was in vain.

Most horrifying was one particular scene. All watched as screaming Jewish children were forcibly taken from their wailing, anguished mothers and burned alive in industrial ovens at the Treblinka concentration camp. Gasps could be heard coming from the audience, even the angels. Many of those in attendance looked at Hitler with murderous contempt. Almost all wept. Shouts of anger echoed through the hall but were gently silenced by the man at the bar.

"I didn't order...I had nothing to do with that," pleaded Hitler.

"No, you did not, but you set those events in motion with your Final Solution," the man said strongly, yet kindly.

He wished again in the innermost chambers of his heart he could simply cease to exist. As more scenes of his crimes and murders played out, guilt as acidic as the soul-pain he experienced in perdition's outer darkness reflexively forbade him from looking at the man at the bar, though he wanted to, for the magnificence of his presence and love enthralled him. He wanted to be with him and bask in that love forever. For one moment, Hitler did force himself to steal a look at the man and to his astonishment sensed there was no vitriol nor judgment emanating from him, only profound sadness and compassion for those who suffered at his hands.

In a moment, the panorama ceased. Every sin, murder, and consequence of action had been shown and discussed by witness after witness. It was mercifully over. There was a slight rustling of commotion as the remaining witnesses were led out of the hall. The man at the bar watched and waited patiently as order was restored. As the final witness exited, he turned toward Hitler.

"Is the punishment you experienced upon your death, during your time in the spirit world and the time in perdition's flame before this judgment and resurrection...was it just?"

"Yes," he answered quietly.

"And the forebodings you feel now of eternal loss and regret...are they also just?"

Hitler stammered and began to weep. Not a sound filled the Judgment Hall. He forced himself again to look at the luminous, incomparable being before him.

"Yes," he choked out between sobs.

"During your long night of suffering, there is one feeling you never felt. Guilt."

Hitler snapped his head upward. In a start he knew he was right.

"The hatred that so characterized your life, the torture of so many innocents, the murders—you never felt true sorrow for your horrible crimes."

"Yes," Hitler meekly offered, nodding.

"Are you sorry for what you did now? If you could, would you make amends? If you lived your mortal life over again, would you make the same choices?" asked the man.

"I...I..."

Infinite shame quashed any ability to speak. The man leaned forward at the bar and placed both his hands on it and patiently waited. After a few moments had passed, in meekness that so characterized him, he asked, "Do you have any final words?"

Hitler fell to his knees. "Yes! I would make amends! I'm sorry. I am so sorry. For everything. I know now how wrong I was. I was wrong! So very, very wrong! Words can't express my shame! Please have mercy on me." He gasped and began to weep uncontrollably.

The man allowed Hitler's words and sobs to again fill the hall. For some, it was agonizingly too long. *Be done with him*, a few of the angels thought. The man heard their thoughts and glanced lovingly yet reprovingly toward them. Then, unceremoniously, the man glanced at the angel who accompanied Hitler to the bar. Having attended innumerable judgments, the angel understood what was to happen next. He circled to Hitler's left and commandingly placed his right hand on the humbled man kneeling before him and looked at the man at the bar as if for instruction.

Hitler knew the angel's presence next to him was meaningful. A terrible dread filled him.

"Stand," the angel commanded with a power Hitler felt compelled to obey. He meekly drew his body upward.

The man removed his hands from the bar and straightened himself. "Very well," he said kindly. "The matter is concluded. Adolf Alois Hitler, by the power of the Holy Priesthood that I hold, I sentence you to the Telestial Kingdom. A place prepared for liars, adulterers, whoremongers...and murderers."

Hitler felt a ripple course through him. Then he drew a stunted breath. In an instant, he had a new body. This one was different from the one he possessed while being judged. It took just a moment to comprehend the change. Something was missing—his genitalia was gone.

With unequaled gentleness, and without a tinge of cruelty, the man at the bar said quietly, "You will never see me again. That is part of your eternal punishment."

"Please no!" Hitler said between sobs.

Anguish as profound as he experienced in perdition's vortex combined with eternal shame filled his soul. Hitler yearned to run to the man at the bar, to tell him he would do anything—anything—to stay with him, but he couldn't move or speak anymore. *Eternal damnation*. Tears rained down his face while a glittering, soundless, white-yellow light enveloped him. He could see the man looking compassionately at him through a small opening in the gathering light, and knew with eternal finality it was the last time.

When the light dissipated, Hitler found himself

standing in front of a modest chalet surrounded by mountains. The scene reminded him of Berchtesgaden in a time so very long ago. The angel who held him in place in the Judgment Hall was with him.

"Where am I? What is this place?" he asked.

"Your final reward," the angel said quietly, taking his hand off his shoulder as he walked around him to face him.

"My reward?"

"Yes. All children inherit something, except for Sons of Perdition, which suffering you undertook for a time. But he is ever generous—even to sinners of your ilk," the glowing angel replied. "And it is far more than you deserve," he added derisively.

Being out of the presence of the man at the bar somehow revived Hitler's spirit. The humiliation and shame that engulfed him were gone, but the consequent emotional devastation of eternal banishment from the man at the bar's presence overwhelmed him. It was an odd juxtaposition to contemplate.

"A soul cannot fail to experience profound guilt in his presence yet his divine love touches each soul in the very marrow of one's being," the angel offered, reading his thoughts and feelings.

"What now?" Hitler asked resignedly after the tumult of emotion passed.

"In a moment. You have paid an exquisite price in suffering for your terrible crimes. Eternal justice has been paid. However, know this: there will always be an abiding sense of loss. Forever. You will have usefulness and blessings even in this lower realm, but you will instinctively know that what you enjoy pales in comparison to what the truly righteous enjoy. And that is a suffering you will always have to endure," the angel said.

"I feel it even now."

"And so you shall for eternity, for you can no longer die. You are damned—like me." The angel said before looking off toward the peaks surrounding them.

"You're damned like me?" Hitler said.

"Yes, but not in the way you think, nor am I like you," said the angel. "Anyone who does not attain exaltation in the Celestial Kingdom where the gods dwell is damned. Damnation means a cessation of individual progress. Exaltation is what the gods enjoy. They are those special souls who overcame all things by faith, learned to love, and kept the law in all things."

"Exaltation?"

The angel cast his eyes downward and picked up his golden staff with both hands before mindlessly moving it upon the ground as if to gather his thoughts.

He continued solemnly, "They become gods. All things are theirs, whether life or death. Powers, glory, love, dominion, principalities, kingdoms, planets, blessings, opportunities, knowledge, wisdom, understanding, family, children, peace, and endlessness are their inheritance. Their glory and blessing are literally beyond your comprehension now. And mine." The angel paused as if to collect himself.

"This is torment not to be in his presence," he blurted out, tears again filling his eyes.

Hitler's comment and emotion seemed to surprise the angel. "Do you not deserve it?" he asked bluntly. "But there is also mercy in that separation. If eternal justice were somehow set aside and you resided in his eternal presence, that would be a punishment more exquisite to you than what you felt at your judgment and in perdition. Do you remember the shattering grief you experienced while being judged?"

"Yes."

"That is what you would feel for eternity. No unclean thing can abide his glory, and you are unclean even though justice has been paid."

The angel brought down his staff hard upon the dirt in finality. "Is there anything else you wish to ask of me before I go?"

"What do I do now? How will I get along? What am I to do?" Hitler asked quietly.

The angel looked at him a long moment with intense yet gentle deliberation. "You will find your way. Goodbye." There was a soundless flash of light and he was gone.

For the first time in an eternity, relief washed over him. After the excruciating crucible he endured in outer darkness, he knew he could tolerate this place, whatever it was. He ran his hands over his body. It was peculiar not having genitalia. In a flash, that now-familiar revelatory intelligence informed him that sexual expression and pleasure were only reserved for the gods in the Celestial Kingdom.

Hitler also knew intuitively that all Telestial Kingdom inhabitants were emasculated. Unlike the endless number of souls who inhabited the lower realm, he didn't care, as sex had never held much interest to him while mortal.

He was now subdued and chastened by his experience in perdition—even grateful. He now found himself willing to comply with moral laws once rejected. Still, an astonishing sense of eternal loss, of what could have been, overwhelmed him.

The bark of a dog disturbed his reverie. Off to his left through a well-manicured garden a German Shepherd bounded toward him. His dog, Blondi. He knelt down and extended his arms.

"Blondi!?" he shouted in surprise.

She joyously bounded toward him and leapt in his arms. He hugged and petted her as the dog happily barked and licked his face.

"I'm so happy to see you, girl!" Hitler said. The dog barked as if in response.

He walked to the porch of his modest chalet and sat on a chair near the door. Blondi sat between his legs as he repeatedly kissed and petted his once-beloved pet. He turned to look into the chalet. In the corner of the room were painting supplies and an easel. And his favorite vegetarian foods on a table in what looked like a kitchen. He smiled. He intuitively knew he didn't need food for his resurrected Telestial body was self-replenishing; it was merely for his pleasure. As were the painting supplies.

He gazed at the wonderment before him. The opalescent sky above was spellbinding. Its hues pulsed with an unearthly, glittering sheen. He watched the sparkling patina of color shift and become iridescent combinations he had never conceived. Just above the mountain to his left, a circumhorizontal arc formed a heavenly kaleidoscope of color. He looked down through the valley before him. To the left was a lake of breathtaking turquoise and azure. To its right, a small village with streets and walkways that glittered becomingly. Snow-capped mountains stood silently overlooking the valley. The scene reminded him of the mountains of Switzerland and Austria from days past. A chilled gust of wind swirled about him. He craned his neck upward to let the breeze bathe his face. With the wind came scents of honeysuckle, pine, and others he knew not. Above him, he could feel the heat of an unknown sun beating down upon his face. He again smiled.

For the first time he could hear the thrum of people in the village below. And music. He again kissed Blondi on the head and rubbed her neck and chest.

"This'll do," Hitler said aloud, quietly. "This'll do."

ON THE SERENGETI, NOTHING IS WASTED

A loud thump awoke Burke Norman. He was not unaccustomed to plane travel, having traversed the globe with his job as a petroleum engineer, but this was different. Ripples of turbulence violently rattled the plane while thick gray and black storm clouds engulfed the Piper Arrow four-seater. He looked out the window to see shafts of lightning crisscrossing the sky as rumbles of thunder mingled with the steady thrum of the engine.

"This is getting bad," said his boss, Ty Charlton, a corpulent, balding man in his mid-sixties.

"I've flown through worse. We'll be fine," said the pilot cheerfully.

The two men exchanged looks at the odd geniality. Burke looked again through his starboard, rain-streaked window when a crackling yellow light enveloped the plane. Numerous sparks sizzled then disappeared, leaving scorch marks on the engine casing. A moment later, all listened as the engine hiccupped and spasmed.

Fear and nausea coursed through Burke as he watched the pilot furiously attempt to re-start the engine, his hands flying over the controls.

"We're losing power. Prepare yourselves for a crash landing," said the pilot.

"Crash?!" shouted Charlton as he grabbed Burke's left forearm. "Do something!"

The pilot radioed the Entebbe International Airport in Uganda, a convenient excuse to avoid the drama in the back seat. Charlton was already whimpering, his face a contorted mask of shock and terror. *We need to know where we are.* Burke hastily grabbed for his calculator in the front pouch of his travel bag lying at his feet.

"What's our average cruising speed been?"

"What?"

"Answer me!" he yelled. "If I know the speed, we can give the tower a more approximate location where we'll land."

"It's 157 mph. But the storm has slowed us down," the pilot offered hastily.

"Distance equals rate times time. Distance equals rate times time," he repeated to himself.

"What are you doing?" Charlton asked, his words dripping with fear.

"Not now." He snapped his head upward toward the pilot, but before he spoke the pilot shouted at him.

"This is good. You can confirm my instruments," he said with the same annoying cheeriness. "Make it three hours, ten minutes."

"Distance is 480.5 miles roughly. There are variables, but that number should be close," Burke shouted aloud.

"Confirmed."

Amid constant static, the pilot relayed the figures to the air traffic controller. Amid the uproar, Burke felt a glimmer of hope but then the radio crackled dead as did the interior lights. An unmanly scream escaped Charlton's lips and the faint smell of urine befouled the cabin. Almost instantaneously the propeller blade slowed then stopped.

"We're going to land somewhere in the Serengeti. Around the north-northeast quadrant," the pilot said.

For the first time Burke detected a hint of fear in the man. He knew what it meant, too. About the size of Northern Ireland, sandwiched between the Kenya border on its east and Lake Victoria on its west, Tanzania's Serengeti National Park was a protected game preserve and wildlife sanctuary housing some of the world's most fearsome predators. Home to over seventy mammals and hundreds of bird species, the Serengeti is a diverse habitat combining woodlands, riverine forests, grasslands and even swamps. The Maasai people dubbed the area "Serengeti" or "endless plains" for its enchanting rolling, grassy expanse. It is also one of the most dangerous places on Earth.

"I'll try to keep it steady and coast as long as I can, but we're rapidly losing altitude and airspeed. We're flying on momentum now," said the pilot, grimly.

"We're going to die!" shouted Charlton.

"Have faith!" the pilot shouted back. "The Serengeti is flat here. If I can control our pitch and roll, we have a chance."

Burke could now see the barren grassland of the Serengeti below. Off to the right, a tower of giraffes huddled together to withstand the storm. Farther still he could see a herd of rhinoceroses as the ground fast approached. A fresh jolt of fear coursed through him as he watched the pilot move a knob downward to retract the landing gear.

"Try to crouch down as low as possible," the pilot said.

Practical matters such as his life insurance policy and

the effect his death would have upon his family raced through Burke's mind. *If we somehow survive the crash, how will we survive the environment?* he thought to himself.

He felt a twinge of guilt for thinking of temporal matters when he saw Charlton's lips move silently in prayer, a blue rosary wrapped tightly around his right hand.

"Get ready! We're at 200 meters...150 meters..." shouted the pilot.

The men in the backseat crouched down just as the plane's wheels touched the earth. For a moment, it was a perfect landing but then the plane shook and rattled as if it were angry. An expletive escaped the pilot's lips. As Burke raised his head above the seat cushion, he understood why. A large African milk tree lay directly ahead. The pilot snapped the steering wheel sharply to port but it was too late. The starboard wing clipped the tree, almost tearing the wing from the fuselage. The wing hung there like an unusable arm scrapping on the grass and dirt before dropping off. The plane veered wildly to the right and banked almost instantly 260 degrees, throwing the plane's inhabitants. A terrifying combination of bangs, screeches, and tearing could be heard as metal wrenched against terrestrial ground. The plane spun another 180 degrees before tumbling onto its starboard side. The tumbling threw Burke against the starboard side window casing, knocking him unconscious. The plane then slid into a protruding, rounded granite rock part of a kopje, a small hilled outcropping of protruding boulders, before terminating its landing with a sickening metallic thud. Only the cockpit, port wing, and landing gear remained intact.

Scattered, disjointed images and sounds greeted Burke, rousing his consciousness. He moaned as he drew his hands upward to massage his throbbing head. A line of blood had flowed and dried from a deep gash over his right eyebrow, accompanied by soreness in his right cheek. An unnatural grogginess overwhelmed him. As he held his eyebrow and forehead with the palm of his hand, he became aware of something lying across his lap. It was Charlton, a smell of urine and excrement filling the air around him. Burke disgustedly pushed him into the groove on the side panel of the fuselage.

"Your boss is dead," said the pilot matter-of-factly as he leaned his upper body against the port door of the cockpit, a red blanket covering his legs. "I checked his pulse numerous times. I think he had a heart attack. He has a few cuts and bruises but otherwise looks fine."

"You're right—he's gone," Burke said heavily as he checked the pulse on Charlton's throat.

"How are you?"

"I hit my head," replied Burke, gently massaging his temples. "I think I have a slight concussion. Other than that, I'm okay. You?"

"My left leg is broken. And a couple of ribs on my left."

"What can I do?"

"What's your name, my friend?" asked the pilot, ignoring the question as rain pattered in a haphazard rhythm upon the cockpit.

"Burke Norman. I'm from the Houston, Texas area."

A middle-aged man of average height with a slightly receding hairline and graying hair, he was once handsome but no more. A quintessential Type B personality, if he hadn't possessed genius-level engineering skill, he would've been just another wispy and forgettable commuter happily ensconced inside a labyrinth of cubicles. That genius however caught the attention of a competing oil company that offered to double his salary and pay off his school loans if he would accept a five-year contract to relocate to Africa. When he initially balked, they also offered free housing and a car. The lure of financial opportunity and debt relief overwhelmed his reticence to travel and adventure, so he agreed.

"Houston's a nice city I hear," the pilot replied politely as if they were meeting each other for the first time at a business conference.

"I suppose," Burke said, as he rubbed his still-throbbing head.

"I'm Felix Kamau from Mombasa, Kenya, although my flying has taken me all over Africa and even Europe occasionally."

For the first time, Burke inspected the pilot. He wore a cream-colored khaki shirt that flopped over whipcord trousers too big for his thin, ectomorphic frame. His face was unremarkable and adorned with abnormally large ears that curved outward, and his teeth were perfectly formed but noticeably yellow, Burke noticed. Wisps of white accentuated his close-cropped black hair as well as his facial stubble. His most remarkable features were his commanding baritone voice and impressive fighter-like forearms. On his right hand, Burke also spied a small cuneiform tattoo that seemed oddly out of place.

"We need to talk my friend. There are some things we need to do to improve our chances of survival. I can't help as I am too injured, but with what I will tell you, it will allow me to pull my own weight," Felix said, slightly smiling, pleased at his turn of phrase.

"Go on."

"You need to drag his body away from here. About 100 meters or so at least." Burke's face grew ashen at the suggestion. "I know what you're thinking but you'll be all right if you do what I say."

"You don't know that."

"Breathe deep, Burki. I know you're scared but I know we can get through this." Only his wife called him Burki. It was peculiar hearing it by this stranger with a Kenyan accent.

"Do you know the best way to drag a body? Put both of your arms under his shoulders and apply a full nelson. Then, walk backward when you drag him," Felix said, gesticulating the movement.

"What about...predators?"

Felix's odd, upbeat manner turned serious. "Yes, I understand. Do you see where the empty dirt meets the grass covering, about 100-120 meters from here?"

Burke looked straight ahead through the plane's window and could see a wide-open area devoid of brush with short straw-like grass.

"Yes."

"Leave him there."

"Why?"

"Because we need to see what animals are close by."

"I don't understand why I need to leave him right there. And now. We should wait till morning."

"We cannot have his dead smell here. It will invite scavengers. We're already intruding on what I believe is lions' territory," Felix said, a touch of impatience seasoning his words.

Felix gently grabbed Burke on the arm.

"I know this is hard, but we are in a fight for our lives, my friend. Make no mistake. If we help each other, we can survive."

After searching through the dead man's belongings for anything useful, Burke watched Felix clumsily exit the cockpit, his head down. He looked left, then right, then turned completely around before shuffling to a small bush ten meters away where a six-to-eight-foot-long stick sat. He shuffled back then placed it against the inactive propeller blade and waited expectantly. Burke took it as his cue to drag the two hundred forty pounds of dead weight from the plane.

"Take off his clothes first. We may need them."

"He soiled himself. His pants stay."

"Fine. Oh, and if a lion or hyena comes near you, throw rocks at them. And make sure you stand your ground. Do you see that stick resting on the propeller blade?" Burke nodded heavily, his glasses already steamed with the heat and exertion. "Take it with you to keep them at bay—if they should approach you."

His eyes nervously scanned and darted in every direction. Bending down, he clumsily secured Charlton again in a full nelson while fighting the disgust of touching the dead body. After righting himself with the corpse, he noisily walked backward, dragging the body toward the area Felix advised. As he progressed, Felix gave him a peculiar two thumbs up sign. At the fifty-meter mark, he fought the urge to stop and rest, but sounds of animals that seemed to come from every direction overwhelmed his fatigue. His breathing was loud and heavy and perspiration rained down his face and neck. He was not as rotund as his erstwhile boss, but years of junk food and a sedentary lifestyle robbed him of any cardiovascular endurance. He arrived at the designated site and gratefully uncoupled himself from the corpse, dropping it heavily to the ground. He paused a moment to catch his breath while his head and eyes again twisted and darted anxiously for signs of life. A refreshing breeze lightly whipped about the plain, a welcome respite. The rain stopped, too, and left a cloudless, clear sky. Along with the breeze came an acrid smell reminiscent of soap but he ignored it and cocked his head down as if praying.

"I'm sorry this happened to you," he said quietly. "You were a good man."

He entertained kneeling and offering a prayer but about two hundred meters away, the high-pitched chuckling sounds of hyenas destroyed any sentimentality. A fresh surge of fear jolted him as he fumbled for the stick before running back to the safety of the plane with a speed that surprised him.

"Well done," said Felix as Burke nervously bent his way into the plane.

They watched as four hyenas circled the body then poked with their noses at the large carcass. It wasn't long before a small committee of vultures arrived, securing themselves on the ground near the sausage tree adjacent Charlton's body. Soon jackals also arrived.

"Why aren't they attacking?" Burke asked.

"They're waiting for the matriarch, the leader of the clan."

Within moments of the vultures' arrival, more cackling vocalizations of a large clan of hyenas could be heard across the open plain. As they came into view, they headed straight to the body, the unearthly glow of their eyes reflecting what light remained in the darkness. Burke's pulse quickened as he watched the pack tear at Charlton's corpse. One female walked off with half of Charlton's arm, and as the hyena snapped her jaw open for a better grip, the hand almost seemed to wave at them. Burke suppressed the urge to wretch but Felix watched impassively, picking his teeth with a toothpick.

A roar announced a large male lion's presence while behind him a large pride of female lions filled out his retinue. The lions were bigger and more beautiful than he expected—and majestic looking. Burke found himself rooting for them as a light skirmish began with the more loathsome hyenas. It was over in minutes. The hair-raising chortling of the last hyena echoed over the plain as it galloped off with Charlton's head in its jaws. The lions watched the final hyena lope away, before descending upon what remained of the carcass. The men watched as the sated lions ambled off, licking each other's faces of blood. Only a few chunks and morsels of Charlton's flesh remained but they were quickly grabbed by the waiting vultures. The men watched as a small African wild dog cautiously peeked its head out of the brown underbrush before sprinting through the kill site and grabbing the spine.

"Quite daring."

"It was over so quickly," Burke gulped.

"Nothing out here lasts."

"He's almost completely gone."

"On the Serengeti, nothing is wasted," Felix replied gravely.

"What now?"

A brief expulsion of air prefaced Felix's reply. "We know lions and hyenas are close by. The hyenas' home base is in that direction about two thousand to three thousand meters away," he said using his head as a pointer to where the hyenas entered the brush. "We *have* landed in the middle of lions' territory."

"I thought they were roaming animals?" Burke said, his heart beating so hard it lifted his shirt.

"Lions are territorial and inhabit the same area for generations."

A long silence passed between them. "What are we going to do?" asked Burke.

"First, we'll catalog our supplies. Behind your headrest there is a large bag. Grab it."

Burke grabbed the dark red bag then rested it on the seat next to him before zipping it open.

The bag proved to be a bonanza. Burke felt his heart lighten each time Felix withdrew his hand. First, he pulled out a 32-ounce bottle of kerosene. Then binoculars, pepper spray, toilet paper, two small buckets, matches, MRE food kits, work gloves, hand towels, duct tape, a few tools, two pots, medical supplies, a hatchet—and bottled water.

"You don't have a satellite phone?"

"They're expensive. We're not as rich as you Americans."

The trip was supposed to be a one-day affair filled with meetings then one night in a hotel before flying back in the morning, but Burke's wife was a notorious over-packer, and he smiled gratefully upon seeing the spate of goods. Snacks, water bottles, and extra clothes filled the handbag. In its corner were capsules of cayenne pepper and bee pollen in a carefully wrapped plastic bag. His wife was on another health kick, he remembered upon seeing them, and insisted upon their use. Felix had only three bottles of water and a small lunch in his suitcase, but the emergency bag made up for it.

The last bag they inspected was Charlton's backpack. They found a few useful items and more food as well as a small hookah and a plastic bag teeming with marijuana. Imagining his strait-laced boss smoking "Mexican tobacco," as his wife called it, evoked a chuckle from Burke.

"That could be useful for my pain management," Felix said, his eyes dancing.

Morning sunlight pierced the windows of the fallen Piper Arrow, rousing its occupants. Though early, the plane's interior was already uncomfortably warm. Both men rose and trudged to a leaf-less bush before baptizing it with a sprinkling.

"You have the pepper spray, yes?" asked Felix knowingly as it protruded visibly outward from Burke's right front pant pocket.

"Yes," Burke said, rapping it gently with the knuckles on his right hand.

"We need to get to the top. Hand me that stick—I'll use it as a crutch."

The top of the kopje was only a few minutes hike for a healthy man, but Felix's injuries slowed them. Upon reaching the top, they were rewarded with a picturesque 360-degree view of the surrounding landscape. The barren land fronting the downed plane was a stark contrast to the rolling plains before them. Roughly a thousand meters to their right lay another kopje three times larger, its numerous boulders rising high above the Serengeti. To their left a combination of green grasses mingled with amber yellow brush. There was no stark demarcation line between desolate and lush, but a gradual blending of arid and fertile. At the horizon line across the northern valley laid a half-formed mountain diffused with distance. To the southeast, zebras peacefully drank from a stream lying next to a towering umbrella tree. In one direction lay numerous trees and waterholes, in another open plains with no variety of plants or even bushes, only gnarled branches and gray pockmarks of dirt.

And the whole plain moved with game. Through his binoculars, Felix saw gazelles, elands, and impala grazing contentedly. Some mingled in and between a massive confusion of wildebeests.

"Do you see that large gathering of wildebeest off in the distance?" Felix said, motioning toward the northeast. Burke used his closed right hand as a makeshift bill to shield his eyes before Felix handed him the binoculars.

"Yes."

"Wildebeest follow a predictable migration pattern. They migrate in a clockwise manner throughout the park, and this is early November." He began talking faster with more energy. "We are most definitely in the northeast section of the park, and that is good news."

"How?" Burke said, returning the binoculars.

"Humans are not natural prey of lions or hyenas. Zebras, wildebeest and gazelles are. There is enough game out there to keep them busy for weeks."

"They ate Charlton."

"Every predator here is a scavenger. If there's an easy

meal to be had, they won't pass it up." Burke nodded in understanding.

"Do you see that tree there?" Felix said, jutting his head in the direction of the large tree casting its shade upon the stream and the zebras.

"It's like this tree here on this kopje."

"It's the tree most associated with Africa. It's called an umbrella tree."

Burke craned his neck to view it. The tree towered over the small outcropping, providing welcome shade in the morning heat. He could also see a few squirrels and rock hyraxes scurrying back and forth on its many limbs.

"Now, that tree to the left about seventy-five meters. See it?"

"Yes," Burke said, breathing out hard through his nose, his non-verbal language conveying his impatience with the botany lesson.

"That is a Balanite or a desert date tree. The fruit is edible raw or cooked and will provide nutrition."

"How do you know so much about this stuff?" Burke asked, changing the subject.

"Don't you think I know my own country and its ways? We breathe with the land. It's a part of us." Loud chirping from squirrels on the umbrella tree's branches disturbed their conversation.

"One last thing. Another reason why I'm certain we are in the northern part of the park is because of a tree the plane hit during the landing. It's called an African milk tree. Do you see it there near the wing?"

The sheared wing was easily identifiable as it gleamed pale yellow in the morning sunlight, a stark contrast to the bleak environment. To its right, Burke could see a large cactus impressive in its width. It had been sliced in half with shards of its remains lying on the ground around gashed earth. It reminded him vaguely of the Saguaro cacti he had seen on a hike in Arizona.

"That's a cactus, not a tree."

"Yes, but it's going to help us a lot, my friend," he said as he readjusted his weight with the makeshift crutch. "It's only in the western and northern parts of the Serengeti. You must gather as much of it as you can so we can put it around, under, and over the plane."

Burke looked at him expectantly.

"Farmers in eastern Africa use it for cattle fencing. Predators won't try to push through it as the stems are dense and poisonous—and sharp."

"Wait! You said 'poisonous'?" Burke asked, his voice rising in pitch.

"Yes. They break apart easily and are full of white, toxic latex. Just one drop can blind you or burn the skin, so be careful."

To protect the skin on his arms, Burke changed into the long-sleeve pullover he secured from his bag and donned the work gloves. After securing the hatchet, pepper spray, and Felix's red blanket, Burke gingerly made his way to the lacerated African milk tree. The plan was to fill the blanket with cacti and drag it back to the plane while Felix stood as look-out.

The remains of the tree stood silently in the middle of the open plain. One hundred meters behind it marked the edge of a field with yellow and gray-brown grass. Only numerous bushes lay between the downed plane and the tree. If an animal exited the cover of the grass, it would serve as an early warning system and provide adequate time to get back to the plane, Felix had said. This gave Burke scant comfort as he hurriedly chopped and gathered cut cacti before carefully placing them on the outstretched red blanket. The work was tedious and slow, and the smell from the night before was even more pungent, but he ignored it. As he dragged the filled blanket of oozing cacti toward the plane, he noticed a white, creamy secretion pasted onto the bushes and grass stalks lining the path.

"These things smell horrible," said Burke as he took a deep swig from a plastic water bottle.

"It's not the cacti," Felix said, wrinkling his nose. "It's the smell of the hyenas' secretions. They've marked this territory."

"Wait, you said this was the lions' territory. How can lions and hyenas share the same area? Do they have an alliance or something?"

"Lions and hyenas hate each other—there is no alliance, I assure you. They regularly compete for prey and ignore the territorial markers of other animals. Quite frankly, we couldn't have landed at a worse spot." Even in the oppressive afternoon heat, Burke felt a chill ripple down his spine.

He also remembered one of the local roughnecks at the plant in Nairobi share an encounter with a spotted hyena pack on a hunting expedition near the Umfolosi Game Park in South Africa. The roughneck droned on about hyenas: their tremendous jaw strength, their ferocity, their nasty dispositions, their cunning.

"They're the outlaws of the Serengeti," the roughneck had sneered.

It took most of the afternoon to chop and gather the remaining cacti. The only animal the men saw was a curious jackal with a distinctive, skunk-like white and black patch of fur on its back. It sat lazily on the gray ground as it scrutinized Burke. It was a beautiful animal with cat-like ears, a fox's face, and a Labrador retriever's body, but he knew it should not be underestimated. As Burke approached the plane with the load of cacti, he gratefully watched it amble off into the underbrush.

"That's the last of it," Burke said with a satisfied tone as he wiped sweat from his brow and face.

"Well done. Before we create the cacti barrier, I want to drain kerosene from the fuel tank," said Felix. "We're going to need it for fires."

The deployed cacti covering the plane and its surroundings looked odd, even comical, but it was functional. Burke watched Felix preparing to start a fire near the front of the plane at the kopje's termination point as he drank greedily from his water bottle.

Weak with the day's exertions, Burke laid on the ground and peered upward at the sky. Darkness had fallen, and with the absence of artificial light, the night sky became a brilliant kaleidoscope of stars and galaxy rim. Any momentary peace was dashed with the macabre combination of snarls and growls and shrieks. The bellows and grunts of lions were easily identifiable, but most unnerving were the vocalizations of the hyenas. Their faux chuckling sounds melded perfectly with the Darwinian environment. Calls of hyenas carry kilometers across the grassland, but he knew they were not kilometers away.

He watched Felix douse the dried wood he had gathered that littered the area with kerosene. They sat on flat boulders ensconced at the front of the cacti-protected plane eating stale MREs while their faces reflected the orange and yellow coloring of the flames.

A streak of movement in the rustling grass near Charlton's final resting place interrupted their dinner. Two jackals sauntered out of the high grass, sniffing the air and ground before them. Burke recognized one of the jackals as the one who had scouted him earlier that day. They circled left then stopped and craned their necks as they took turns yowling high-pitched calls that were immediately answered deep within the savannah. Moments later the distinctive calls of hyenas echoed over the barren grassland. Burke grabbed a few rocks the size of a man's hand and the lone bottle of pepper spray.

"The fire will keep them at bay. They don't know what it is. If they try to test the cacti perimeter, they'll lose interest, I think," Felix said.

"You think?"

Burke watched in astonishment as Felix impassively resumed eating as if he were sitting on a Barcalounger watching a movie. The jackals were soon joined by three brindle-colored hyenas. Their glowing eyes in the sparse light coupled with their unearthly high-pitched chuckling unnerved Burke. He watched them dart in an uneven pattern across the plain before them. The jackals gave their competitors a wide berth, but the hyenas charged them repeatedly as if to remind them that this was their territory.

Both species seemed curious about the men as they eyed them across the plain. A muffled growl to the right near the shorn African milk tree caused man and animal to snap their heads toward its origin. Two lionesses casually strolled through the grass, making a wide turn past the tree. They entered the open field, their attention solely on the hyenas. The larger of the lionesses raised her left cheek letting out a low menacing growl. As they approached, both lions swished their tails back and forth vigorously like a domesticated house cat.

"They're interested in the hyenas, not us," Felix deadpanned. "Look at their tails. That means they feel threatened. When lions hunt, they stay as still as possible."

"So! They're lions! Why aren't you more concerned about this?" Burke whispered in near panic.

"Calm down. If they charge us, stand your ground and throw rocks at them. And don't turn your back to them," he said while stirring embers in the fire with a stick. "They need to know we're not afraid of them. This was inevitable."

Burke watched the lions intensely but Felix was right—their attention was solely on the hyenas. They formed a semi-circle around the big cats who countered by charging in a burst of dazzling ferocity. Two of the hyenas scampered off, but the remaining hyena darted in at one of the lions' hindquarters, its nip drawing blood. The big cat whirled and roared in pain, its ears pinned back in anger. It charged, sinking its teeth deep into the offending hyena's neck as it wrestled it to the ground. A high-pitched yelp of pain came from the downed animal as the other lioness joined the scrum.

The speed and ferocity of the attack left Burke breathless and awestruck. The lioness grabbed the dead hyena by the neck and casually sauntered back through the field. One of the jackals darted in to grab a quick mouthful but an angry charge by the other lioness forced it to sprint off.

"What game are you playing at? You're wounded. We have limited resources. We're lost. And we have no weapons other than pepper spray and a walking staff. And you think we can fight them off," Burke said, his hands trembling.

"We can't waste food out here. Eat," Felix said as he put the last mouthful of MRE into his mouth.

"I'm not hungry!" Burke barked as he sat down and tried to get his breathing under control. After a beat passed, he glanced up at the star-filled night sky. "We're going to die out here, aren't we?"

The cooing of African doves in the kopje's umbrella tree awoke Burke. He laid in the back seat curled in a ball, his stomach already queasy. After a few minutes, his middle-age stiffness dissipated, encouraging him to arise. He rubbed his face and looked out the window and could already see shimmering heat radiating upward from the ground like it was a hot plate. A clanking on the port door disturbed his trance.

"Ready for some breakfast?" Felix asked cheerfully while zipping open Charlton's backpack. It was filled to the top with nuts.

"You went out there by yourself?"

"We are most fortunate that tree is there. I also saw another. We will have no problem with food," he said. Burke noticed Felix's pattern of ignoring questions he didn't want to answer.

"What about water?"

"Water is good," he said, his pronunciation garbled due to a mouth filled with nuts. He reflexively put another into his mouth before responding. "But we will both have to go to that watering hole to the southeast today."

The thought was instantly unappetizing to Burke, who smelled the unfamiliar date-sized nut before taking a tentative bite. Its sweet earthy flavor surprised him. He ate nut after nut contentedly as Felix peppered him with instructions for their outing to the stream.

It was no easy task. They first had to move the cacti aside to exit the perimeter. Then they had to replace it without touching the needle-sharp, spikes or white latex ooze already dried in the African sun.

Felix checked the backpack one last time while Burke surveyed the cacti and the immediate surrounding area around the plane for animal tracks. They rounded a small grove of young umbrella trees and came upon a small dazzle of zebras peacefully drinking from the stream. At the far end a small herd of gazelles noiselessly grazed on the patches of grass. The zebras stopped drinking to watch them, their tails flicking nervously.

"There are no crocodiles or else one of the zebras would've been taken by now, but stir the water and watch for movement anyway before dipping the pail and bottles. And prepare to move quickly backward just in case. They are astonishingly fast when snatching prey."

Burke did as instructed. The thought of being eaten alive by a crocodile was more frightening in his imagination than death by a lion or hyena. With the first bucket secured, Burke poured it over himself, then Felix. It was a welcome refreshment in the unabating heat. They took a few moments to splash themselves with the water and drink their fill before filling the bottles with the water from the buckets. As Burke finished filling the final bottle, the zebras on the plain began chortling excitedly. Coming toward the men in a casual gallop were five hyenas; behind them fifty meters back, were four fast-walking jackals. Burke anxiously handed the final water bottle to Felix, who dropped it into the backpack.

"This may not have been a good idea," Felix said while fumbling through the backpack for the pepper spray.

"What choice did we have?" said Burke, his temples pounding so hard it distorted his vision.

"Don't turn your back to them. Stay as close to the edge of the water as possible and then near the trees as we make our way back. They're pack hunters—they'll try to encircle us."

It was slow going, as Felix's broken leg hampered any speed. But as the hyenas approached, they unexpectedly veered off toward the scrambling zebras. But not the jackals. They followed the men back to the plane and watched intently while Burke painstakingly moved aside the cacti fronting the entranceway to the plane.

"That wasn't too bad," said Felix as the port door clanked shut.

He rubbed his hands together as if to warm them. Burke was content to lean against the back corner of the seat and breathe. They watched as the jackals tentatively maneuvered their way inside the layered cacti perimeter but gave up when pricked by the sharp spines. It was an easy decision to stay in the plane the rest of the day.

As the afternoon abated, the men left the safety of the cab to relieve themselves and stretch their legs but were interrupted by a high-pitched sound vaguely reminiscent of a malfunctioning trumpet. Off to the northeast, through the flickering heat and rising dust plumes, they saw a dazzle of restless zebras dotting the plain. Without warning, a streak of golden-brown emerged from the low grass toward a grazing zebra on the outer edge of the dazzle's perimeter.

The men watched as the zebra abruptly changed direction repeatedly in a desperate effort to escape before the lioness clipped its hind leg, causing it to stumble before being wrestled to the ground. It was simply no match for the big cat's speed and agility. Seven other lionesses joined in the fight, the largest of the pride wrapping her mouth around the zebra's throat. Overwhelmed by the superior force, the zebra quickly tired. Even from their distance, the men could see the other lionesses tearing at the stomach and hindquarters while it was still alive. In a moment the frantic twitching of its legs stopped.

The male lion ate first, devouring the organs, then the females clustered around the prey in a concentric circle, feeding with their young. Within moments, a clan of hyenas appeared, then vultures and marabou storks who took their place at the outer ring of the kill site. Then jackals and African wild dogs sauntered in. All patiently waited their turn. Except the hyenas.

They snarled and snapped at the male lion's hindquarters in an attempt to draw him off. He raised his head to ascertain the threat, its face smeared with blood and eyes wide with intensity. He snarled at the offending hyena, but then resumed gorging on the fresh meat. Two lionesses weren't as patient. They veered off their places at the carcass to growl and snap at the circling hyenas before rejoining the kill.

"They're brave, I'll give them that," said Burke.

"In some ways they're more formidable than lions. A

hyena can smell blood twenty kilometers away."

Days passed. Burke put his engineering skills to work by fashioning a makeshift cast out of duct tape and umbrella wood for Felix's broken leg. The area around the broken ribs was more troubling—its magenta and mulberry coloring was spreading. The cayenne helped but they both knew it was only a stopgap measure. An aura of desperation mixed with the decaying smell of the leg—both knew time was running out. Felix leaned heavily against the port door and craned his head to look through the cockpit window at the purple streaks filling the twilight sky.

"How are our supplies?" he asked heavily.

"The bee pollen is gone; so are the MREs. The only food left are the nuts. But we're almost out."

"And the water?"

Burke rubbed and massaged his face with both hands before responding. "We need more of that, too. But we're good for the night. In the morning, I'll get more of both."

"You're getting used to this place, aren't you?"

"I'm still scared."

"So am I, my friend," Felix said solemnly.

"What are we going to do? You need medical attention and we can't live on nuts and unfiltered water forever."

Felix raised himself in his seat carefully to avoid any twinge of pain. "I need your attention."

Burke looked at him intently. A long beat passed between them.

"You have to go get help." The words hung in the stifling air as both knew its implications. Burke looked down a long time before wiping the sweat off his forehead and arms, but it was just busywork to fill time.

"I won't last a day out there and you know it."

"It's been done before."

"Hike through the Serengeti? Alone? That's your idea?"

"There is a road, I think, about ten kilometers from here that is used for tourists. If you can find that, follow it northeast," Felix said.

"You're talking as if I've agreed to this. I'm not going out there!" Burke said as he ran his hands through his thinning hair.

"I don't think they're looking for us anymore," Felix said with deadly earnestness as he looked at the horizon. "We have to press the issue."

"I'm going outside," Burke said, wanting to be done with the conversation.

After the incident at the waterhole, he always left the plane with the work gloves and the hatchet. He moved the cacti to the side, then looked around for signs of life and saw only a few squirrels. Burke watched as one artfully traipsed its way around the cacti on the roof of the plane before shimmying down the plane's starboard side to retrieve a few discarded desert date tree nuts Felix had casually tossed away on their last water run. They eyed each other a moment before the squirrel turned the nut over and over in its fingers as if it were inspecting it. Other than the squirrels, the cacti had worked. Even the jackals were avoiding it. The jackals returned a few days after their first unsuccessful foray into the perimeter, but after hearing a succession of loud yelps then frustrated snarls, Burke watched them run off into the underbrush. A welcome breeze floated through him as he eyed the sloping mountain in the smoky, late afternoon haze.

"I thought this was supposed to be the rainy season," Felix said in his typical upbeat manner. Burke offered a polite scoff. He was almost used to his clothes sticking to him in the steamy heat.

"Only if our luck changes."

Behind him he heard Felix noisily grabbing the smooth, rounded rocks lining the outcropping to encircle the fire pit.

"The nuts are actually quite good toasted," Felix said. "It's unfortunate we don't have any cinnamon to go with them."

A few of the squirrels sat on the boulders above them watching expectantly. Burke grabbed the hatchet and a few palm-sized rocks before making his way to a large bush fifteen meters from the plane.

A scream pierced the air.

Burke hastily zipped his pants then grabbed the hatchet as he darted out from behind the bush. As he ran, a swell of shock colored his world: attached to Felix's left triceps was a black mamba at least four meters in length. Felix grabbed its neck just below its coffin-shaped head as Burke chopped down its body. The pain caused the snake to let go of Felix's arm who pushed its head down into the flat rocky outcropping. Burke carefully secured the snake at its neck just below its head then smashed it with the blunt end of the hatchet.

"Listen to me. I don't have much time," Felix gasped as he fell forward into Burke's arms.

"Let me suck some of the poison out—it'll help! And the cayenne, there's a little cayenne left! It might help, too," Burke said frantically, cradling Felix's upper body and head in his arms.

"There's nothing that can be done. I have fifteen minutes at best." His breathing was already shallowing as he convulsed in pain. "If you live, promise me you'll visit my family. Tell them I loved them; tell them..."

"You have my word."

"You have to hike out of here. I know you can do it. You're tougher than you think. Promise me."

"I will."

"Burki, always remember: life is very beautiful even when it's not," he said with a tone of finality and sentimentality that jarred him. He held him, rocking him gently until his friend's breathing slowed to nothingness.

Burke created a makeshift torch out of strewn sticks near where the dead snake's body lay. He flung it away in frustration and let out a loud yawp that filled the plain. Tears filled his eyes and slithered down his cheeks as he dragged Felix's remains to the same spot where he had left Charlton. Remains of Charlton's shredded pants and shirt still remained but nothing else. It filled him with anger for some reason. This time he prayed a moment over his friend. But didn't linger. Within minutes, he heard the damnable high-pitched cackling of the hyenas. He again watched in horror as the entire clan loped through the thigh-high graying grass and descended upon Felix's remains. Within minutes the parade of other carnivores also arrived. He silently watched from the safety of the plane, emotion overwhelming him. He preferred the lions eat his friend, not the loathsome hyenas. Somehow it was more dignified. Everything about them disgusted him: their shuffling, sideways gait and human-like laugh, their mottled appearance. *The outlaws of the Serengeti.*

It was strange being alone in the cabin, and so final. He had come to like the man—even his insufferable cheeriness. The queasiness in his stomach was a constant companion throughout the evening as he planned the trip to the tourist road. After another kerosene run, he re-filled the main kerosene bottle and used two of the water bottles for the overflow. Fire would be essential to his survival. The stark reality of his situation was clarion clear: he would need to traverse forty to seventy kilometers—on foot—through terrain filled with deadly carnivores, and do it with limited sleep. Felix told him repeatedly the one cardinal rule of the Serengeti—don't sleep unless you have someone or something to guard you. If he were lucky, he could climb a tree and tie himself to it for a few hours of precious sleep. But he knew lions climbed trees as did cheetahs and snakes. The thought of snakes was a fresh wound. He grabbed the binoculars to look where Felix last lay, but he was already gone.

The predators on the Serengeti were nocturnal hunters, so he would rise early and go first light. He would go to the stream and fill the water bottles, then to the desert date tree and fill the backpack with nuts. The other bags would be filled with other essentials for survival. After sharping the ax and knife, he finished packing the bags and slipped into a deep sleep.

The alarm from his wrist-watch intruded upon his consciousness. The thinning black of night in the east told him dawn was approaching. He knew he must traverse as much distance as possible before the heat of the day descended. As he lighted out of the plane, fresh, cool air caressed his face as did the smell of early morning. He relieved himself and surveyed the area for activity. Off to the north he heard zebras honking and the high-pitched cooing of wildebeests, but there were no predators.

As he approached the stream, any lingering fatigue was exorcised upon seeing a herd of water buffaloes drinking thirty meters upstream. They eyed him curiously, their ears twitching and mouths moving side to side as if they were chewing gum. He remembered Felix saying they were among the most dangerous of African mammals on the Serengeti. Their appearance was unsettling. And they looked exactly as Felix described them. They were heavily muscled with sharp horns that parted down the middle of their heads and extended outward. "They have aggressive dispositions, especially when threatened," he could hear Felix saying in his mind.

"I assure you if you leave me alone, I'll leave you alone," Burke whispered to himself as if it were a spell.

A few stamped their feet and bellowed but settled with his presence. He filled the water bottles, and though it was early morning, doused himself in anticipation of the coming savannah heat.

The water buffaloes watched him impassively as he gathered his backpack and bags before retreating toward the desert date tree. Most of the nuts had already been stripped away so he made his way to the second tree Felix said was a hundred meters east. It wasn't. He dug out the pocket binoculars from his pants' front right pocket and surveyed the area. The tree was difficult to identify in the early twilight, but he found it standing silently on the edge of amber-colored grass.

For the first time he saw the trail of cut earth where

the plane crashed. Gashed earth and debris littered the path including the starboard landing gear. He surveyed it for usefulness but didn't linger—he reminded himself he must hike fifteen to twenty-five kilometers before sundown.

The proximity of the tree to the knee-high grass was unnerving but necessity dominated his reality. He held the backpack to his chest and zipped it open when he heard a rustling in the grass. He nervously reached for the axe hanging through a loop on the backpack when something heavy and powerful fell soundlessly on his back and wrapped its paws around his chest. The claws dug deep into him as fangs clamped onto his skull. The pain was horrifying, real. He swung the ax hard into its side, causing the animal to retract and growl in pain but only for a moment. Its weight and strength forced him to the ground, knocking the ax out of his hand. As he fell, he saw what was attacking him—lions.

Another smaller lioness clamped her jaw around his neck as the other held him down. Two others scampered through the grass adjacent the tree and joined the kill. One gnawed at his stomach and another bite down on his left thigh but a squirt of blood to its face from his punctured femoral artery startled it. Fear and panic staggered his consciousness.

He could feel the hot breath of the lions on his throat and the sickly-sweet smell of decay from its breath. The mind's mischief was always at play—even in the final throes of life. An arcane thought from a book read years ago flashed through his mind—*death is an experience that is lived through*. The sheer terror of being eaten alive sharpened his awareness. Off in the distance, he heard the roar of the pride's dominant male pierce the air.

A fresh surge of fear caused him to claw and gouge with his hands, the only weapon remaining to him. He succeeded in digging his nails and thumbs deep into the eyes of the lioness suffocating him, causing her to recoil with a growl.

She determinedly lunged back at his throat and secured it tightly with another rumbling, guttural snarl. He could feel his stomach tearing open. The loss of blood from his femoral artery caressed his senses, bringing a gradual but blessed unconsciousness. *Dear God, I love my family.*

That was the last thought of the man known as Burke Norman. No sooner had it coursed through his brain when there was a loud snap of bone. As his body went limp, the entire pride descended upon his ample flesh. The male dove into the stomach region of the now redly flesh and devoured most of the organs before walking off as it licked its blood-stained face. A lioness immediately occupied the space vacated and lounged at the liver, devouring it. The rest of the pride orderly gorged upon other ample areas of meat left by the male, including the buttocks and back. There was no sentiment, no reasoning. Only behavior dictated by chemical instinct. What lay before them was opportunity to sate hunger. Nothing more.

The kill attracted the attention of the other predators on the savannah. The hyenas uncharacteristically waited a respectful distance from the kill site, content to wait for the lions. Vultures occupied the next ring, then the jackals and wild dogs. At the outer-most, marabou storks.

Off to the side of the kill site on the now mated, blood-colored ground, laid Burke Norman's head. The site was covered with blood and chunks of flesh and bones, but the head was left intact, save for the holes made by the lion's tusks and a large gash below the left eye. The eyes remained open and blank, staring into space, a horrified look filling them. A young hyena cautiously scampered in and grabbed it without attracting the lions' attention before it darted off through the grass. Within minutes, it, too, was consumed.

The honking and chortling of zebras and wildebeests nearby proved irresistible to the impatient clan of hyenas who galloped off for easier prey. Moments later, the lions ambled away. As the last of the pride disappeared through the amber grass, the vultures descended. The birds gorged and squawked restlessly, even fighting a macabre tug-of-war over what had been cartilage in Burke Norman's left knee. With the remaining flesh now gone, the vultures flew off *en masse* to find other carrion. The jackals then trickled into the kill site and nibbled the remaining carcass clean. One dashed off with half of a ribcage in its mouth as if it were a souvenir; any scant remains were quickly devoured by the hungry jackals. When the jackals left, only a few meager fragments tarried in the early morning sun, including a small piece of flesh that had somehow fallen into the open backpack near the date nut tree, where it was found by a hungry marabou stork who swallowed it. The encrusted blood and morsels remaining were licked off the matted earth by flies and wild dogs.

The man was gone. Obliterated. Digested into nothingness. All that remained were his intestines whose pungent scent caught the attention of dung beetles and flies. Never in the thoughts of the bipedal organism known as Burke Norman was it conceived that his excrement and intestinal mucoid plaque would become the walls of a small colony of African dung beetles. But thus it was.

The meaty flesh and bones commingled in the stomachs of the satisfied pride of lions and other scavengers, the flesh dissolving into amino acids and other nutrients needed for life. As evening fell, what hadn't served as nutrition for the carnivorous predators of the Serengeti was eliminated where it silently decomposed into the brown, indifferent earth. But it, too, in time, would bequeath something to the dance of life upon the African plain.

Because on the Serengeti, nothing is wasted.

KING BILLY THE WICKED

On my first day as a newly minted high school English teacher, he was the first student who sauntered into my classroom, and although I didn't know it then, I would remember him forever. I was immediately struck by how handsome he was. He had an easy smile and a genuine warm manner—and he was skinny. African-marathon-runner-skinny.

He was a troubled boy and it was easy to see why. His father was a womanizer and an alcoholic who routinely beat him. After his father left, his deadbeat mother supported him with welfare, and perhaps most painful of all, both sides of his extended family shunned him. Later I'd heard a story that his own grandmother told him to his face that he was a "pig." Ostracized and demeaned at every turn, he became a loner.

He was one of only five white kids in the high school with two of the five his sisters. In all my classes, there were forty kids, about twenty-five too many. The students were predominantly Black and Hispanic, with a few Filipinos and Asians, and one white student. Billy was that white student.

He often came to school with bruises on his arms and face. I don't think I ever saw him without a fat lip. At first,

I thought it was because of beatings at home but I was wrong—he was bullied. And terribly so. It was only later I discovered how unrelenting it was. Others were harassed, but he was the favorite target. He was a perfect foil, too: poor and quiet. Just one of those reasons would've been enough but he was also exceptionally bright. Preternaturally so. And everyone knew it. The math teacher told me Billy could do high-level math equations in his head, and the Spanish teacher said he spoke fluent Spanish after only a summer of study. As his English teacher, he impressed me as well. Though he made few comments in class, he exhibited a formidable vocabulary and demonstrated an expansive understanding of linguistic device. His command of grammar and punctuation was so nuanced, he actually—and gentlemanly so as befitting his mien—pointed out a subject-verb error I made on the mid-term instructions. He was also astonishingly well-read and in his class assignments routinely quoted Benjamin Franklin, Shakespeare, and Marcus Aurelius. During one of the few times he spoke in class, he even quoted the unreadable Immanuel Kant to bolster an opinion, which brought a fresh surge of ridicule. His writing, too, was soulful and expressive well beyond his years.

He was also a peculiar creature of habit, which only lent itself to his natural charm. His light brown hair was always coiffed with gel in the same way. And he always sat in the same place—the corner seat closest to the back door so he could immediately leave upon the final bell. He would always enter and leave through that door, and was always early. He would enter alone through the back door as it minimized contact with the other students, and he would then sit quietly rifling through the assigned textbook as he waited for class to begin. It was his way of saying he didn't want to talk.

His attire was especially habitual. He only wore faded jeans, white athletic socks, and T-shirts. His color scheme was always charmingly predictable, too. On Mondays, he wore black T-shirts, on Tuesday, white. Wednesdays were for French blue, Thursdays, green. And on Fridays, burgundy. He never deviated from that regime. Near the end of the school year, he began wearing only wrinkle-free white T-shirts. Sometimes they were long-sleeved, but they were always white. A pristine white. An unearthly white. So much so, I wondered if he ironed and bleached them. That change in routine would be the only warning sign.

He also had a curious nickname: the kids called him King Billy the Wicked. Even the bullies. It was bestowed grudgingly and would be the only homage of friendship ever given.

Before the start of class in the early autumn, Billy hadn't yet come in so I asked one of the more popular girls how he'd acquired such an unusual moniker. Her eyes widened as she drew in a deep breath while snapping her gum the way only a sixteen-year-old girl can.

"Because he's the king on the court, Miss Williams. He. Is. The. King. Even the brothers admit it." Two of the African-American boys sitting at the back of the class nodded vigorously in agreement, their eyes widening.

"Really?" I asked dumbfounded. "Billy. Our Billy?"

"Oh yeah," chimed in one of the boys.

"On the basketball court," I stammered, not really believing. "Billy." They laughed at my disbelief.

"He's got game. He's *really* quick, can pass, jump, shoot, you name it."

"If you're open, he'll find you," added the other boy.

"Oh yeah. He's the man. That's why some of the boys hate him," the girl added. "It started as 'King Billy the Wicked Smart,' but then it got shortened when people saw how good he was at basketball."

"KB's good at baseball, too," added the boy sitting on the window-sill between slurps of a blue slushy. "He's got a gun for an arm and can run like a deer."

I helped the lunch lady change a flat tire during my second month at the school. She was a corpulent Samoan woman with one eyebrow and the charm of a golden retriever. I liked her instantly. She said if I changed her tire, she'd owe me a favor. Afterward, while she put away the hydraulic trolley and wrench in her trunk, I asked her to give free school breakfast and lunch to Billy in perpetuity as payment.

"The good-looking boy. King Billy?" she asked as she wiped her meaty hands of grease.

"Yes," I answered, surprised she knew his nickname.

Sexual attraction and pity joined to form a peculiar facial expression on her round, double-chinned face. "He's a pretty boy," she said, almost conspiratorially.

She snapped her head up, catching herself. "I'll arrange it."

After a few months passed, I told Billy I wanted to see him after class. His good looks caught me off guard a moment as he sashayed toward my desk. I was only twenty-two then—I had to remind myself he was my student and that I was engaged. He had the timidity of someone who had been terribly wounded, and was ever-deliberate in his responses, but it only made him more endearing to me. After a few minutes of talking, I almost forgot how handsome he was as his native warmth and intelligence crept through.

"You're too skinny. You need to eat better," I remembered saying, surprised at my candor.

He looked down at his worn Chuck Taylor All-Stars with those Elizabeth Taylor blue eyes and mumbled, "We're poor. But I'm okay."

"You sure?" I asked.

He looked out the glass windows to his left then mindlessly rolled my stray red grading marker back and forth on my desk before looking at me. "Miss Williams, I know what you did with the lunch lady and all. I wanted to thank you."

"You're welcome," I said, my heart aglow. He offered a polite smile as he slung his backpack around his right shoulder before ambling out.

Most days of our lives are meaningless. Only a few leave an impact. I know mine. The day I got married, the day I graduated from college, the day my mom died, the birth of my first child, and the day Billy changed my life forever. I was sitting at my desk grading papers as students filtered in. The room buzzed with conversation between the students waiting for class to start. I watched slightly amused as one of the Hispanic kids politely, yet strongly, inform one of the Asian boys he couldn't sit in a certain seat. Even though there were no assigned seats, everyone sat in the same section, and everyone knew it was verboten to sit in an unauthorized area. The Black kids all sat in the three rows adjacent the windows with the leaders of the group occupying the back seats. The Asian and Filipino students took the upper-right and front, the Hispanics the middle. On this day, Billy was late, and he was never late.

The class moaned audibly as I announced an unplanned vocabulary quiz. As I rose to hand out the quizzes, out of the corner of my eye, I thought I saw Billy's coiffed hair through the small rectangular window of the closed rear door. As I handed out the papers to the students in the front rows, I heard a repeated banging at the foot of the door. Even then I didn't think anything was wrong, it was only peculiar. But what happened next wasn't. I asked a boy who sat to Billy's immediate left to find out what was making the sound. He stood on his toes to look through the window when almost instantly, black spray paint filled it.

"It's King Billy," the boy said.

I turned to drop the extra quiz papers onto my desk when Billy, shirtless, burst through the door nearest my desk. I was surprised by that but before I could say anything, he tossed a green apple to me, which I instinctively caught. One of the bullies who terrorized him so relentlessly said something as he entered but I don't remember what. I don't know why, as everything else that happened on that day I recall with perfect clarity. After the bully's comment, a froth of laughter rippled through the class. Billy savagely turned to the boy in the corner and told him to shut up with a ferocity I had never seen in him. The Billy I knew was always so meek and mild, but this Billy I didn't recognize.

It was then I noticed the gun in his right hand. A few of the girls stifled a scream and the rest a gasp. Fear was in everyone's face, even the bullies.

"Billy, calm down. It'll be okay, I promise," I said not quite believing what I was seeing.

"Anyone makes a sound or tries to go out through the windows, you die," he said ferociously before turning slightly aback to the class.

He methodically turned the lights off with his left hand then stuck a wooden door jamb into the base of the door. He put the gun down in front of him before he retrieved a hammer he had stuffed into the back of his jeans. He struck the jamb three or four times until it was embedded into the soft ecru tile. As he had with the rear door, he spray painted the door's window black before dropping the can to the floor where it clanked noisily before rolling to a stop against the wall.

Facing the class, he then pushed my wooden desk back with his buttocks until it was flush against the blackboard. I retreated to the right corner of the room not sure what to do. Even then I felt I could calm him down. He ordered me to sit on the floor, and I did so. I thought I knew at that moment what he planned, but I was wrong. It was as if time stopped along with my heart and breath.

"Billy, please! Don't do this! You're so gifted, so talented. You have something special that the world needs to see. I know they bully you. They're not worth it. Please don't," I said.

"Yet you never did anything about it, did you?" he said, his words like a javelin to my heart.

He then palmed the gun like policemen on television and pointed it at the boys who terrorized him. One by one, he ordered the four bullies by name to stand in front of the windows.

"He won't do nothing," one of them sneered.

Billy shot a bullet at the ceiling, provoking a startled scream from the Asian and Hispanic girls bunched together at the back of the room.

"Do it!" Billy yelled.

The four boys came out from the clustered crowd at the back of the class. They gingerly spread out along the heater fronting the windows. He took a step back and deliberated with indecision. It didn't occur to me at the time but each of the four bullies who tormented him were all outstanding athletes with tremendous promise. Two played basketball, one football, the other baseball. All were heavily recruited by Division I schools for scholarships in their respective sports. The boy who played baseball was projected as a first-round draft pick in the upcoming Major League Baseball draft where he would make millions if he opted not to go to college. He was a highly prized left-handed pitcher who was believed to be the next Randy Johnson, I remembered reading later.

"Billy, I'm sorry, man. I'm sorry," said one of the boys who played basketball. The other boys said nothing, their faces contorted in a combination of disdain and fear.

I'd never seen him play basketball, but I could see the athletic skill and focus I had heard about as he fired into his tormentors. The boy to the far right he shot first, once in each knee, in the stomach, then in each shoulder. He did the same with the other two. As the last clip expired, he dropped it and skillfully re-loaded the gun with a clip he retrieved from his back left pocket as if he had done it a hundred times. The heavily recruited baseball player thought he could get to him, but Billy was too fast. He shot him as he had the others but then paused before he shot him three times in the left arm—twice in the shoulder and once in the elbow. I watched, open-mouthed, my head spinning, as the boys writhed on the ground in pain, their bodies covered in blood.

I've often wondered why he let them live, why he shot them the way he did. I think I know. Billy knew the shots wouldn't kill them, but it would damage them the way he'd been damaged. He wanted them to know the desperation and grief he felt. He wanted to take something from them the way so much had been taken from him. He wanted to destroy the boys' dreams the way his had been destroyed.

The Hispanic and Asian kids huddled together in front of the rear door. Almost all were whimpering and crying in fear. I saw him glance in their direction for a moment but he said nothing. At that moment, out of the ether beyond my ken of understanding or awareness, a strange thought suddenly dropped into my mind: King Billy the Wicked spoke in class today. The thought was right—he spoke. Not in words, but in actions that would leave an indelible imprint upon all who were there that day.

Shouts and havoc could be heard outside the doors as he calmly faced the windows. He looked longingly at the morning sun and blue sky as if they were made just for him. And maybe they were. I couldn't see his entire face, just his right profile. It was then I saw a tear trickle down his right eye and roll down his cheek.

He turned to his right to face me as I sat huddled against a gray metallic file cabinet, my arms wrapped around my drawn-in knees. I saw his entire face suddenly. Tears coursed down it in large droplets before they fell to the tile. Movies have conditioned us to think people routinely weep tears that roll down their face. But it isn't so. Such tears are born of pain few will ever know. To weep so, one must be consumed by an all-encompassing grief that melts the very soul. I've only seen such tears once, and it was on that day. He looked at me most pitifully as he struggled for words. Something went cold in the world at that moment and in all who saw what happened next.

"King Billy the Wicked will never rule the world," he haltingly said as he put the gun barrel to his right temple.

I wanted to quit teaching. But after a trip to Italy over summer break, and talks with my fiancée, Otis, I changed my mind. Principal Robinson told me she'd do whatever she could to get me to come back, even offering counseling and a raise.

"I want another classroom," I blurted out. "I can't..."

"I understand. It's yours," she said, hugging me as I cried.

I took the counseling, and it did help somewhat. But nothing will erase the events of that day from my memory's blackboard. From then on, every year, on the first day of school, and whenever I felt it was needed, I gave a lecture on bullying and the worth of each student. I think it made a difference. I hope it did. God knows.

The four bullies came to predictable ends. The football player became a thief and alcoholic before killing himself a few years later. In his suicide letter, he apologized for his role in Billy's death. He would be the only one. The baseball player was killed in a bar fight in Cancún. He never played a day of college or professional ball and spent the rest of his life unable to lift his left arm. The other two remained friends and were found shot dead in what police described as a "drug-related incident." I feel no pity for them. Maybe it was the universe righting a wrong. I hope it was. Billy deserved better. So did the world.

I'm retired now. I'd like to think I was a good teacher. The vast majority of my students flitted away into obscurity as most of us do. A few did noteworthy things. One became a national broadcast journalist of some renown, another an author. None of them were as talented or as gifted as Billy, though. And yes, I'm still haunted by the tragedy of that day. I'm haunted by the grief I saw in Billy's eyes. I'm haunted for not doing more. I'm haunted by what he could've been. I'm haunted.

Because King Billy the Wicked will never rule the world.

THE GREATEST HITTER WHO EVER LIVED

Bright light and sounds of machines amid overlapping voices pierced the deep slumber of the lanky man on the medical table. A biting cold, metallic taste in his mouth overwhelmed him as did the burning in his nostrils. He forced his eyes open to a squint. Everything and everyone seemed aglow in a dazzling white light like an angel in a Carl Bloch painting.

"Am I in...Heaven?" he mumbled softly, the words creaking out.

The thought itself was jarring. Baseball legend Ted Williams had faith in science, not religion. His will stated he be cremated and the ashes scattered over the Florida Keys where he spent countless hours deep-sea fishing. But while in the hospital awaiting an angiogram in November of 2000, his children, John-Henry and Claudia, persuaded him to be cryogenically frozen after death. The day after he died of congestive heart failure, his corpse was flown to the Alcor Life Extension Foundation in Scottsdale, Arizona where he was placed in cryonic stasis. Where it would remain, he was assured, until technology evolved for eventual resurrection.

A scant two years after Williams' passing, his son John-Henry died of leukemia and had his remains cryonically suspended and tubed alongside him. In 2042, Claudia joined them.

"No, Mr. Williams," softly chuckled the man. "Please choose calmness. I am promising all your questions will be answering. Right now, choose breathing deeperly and relaxing."

The strange non-idiomatic English caught his attention but a weak nod was all he could muster.

He noticed something else, too: everyone was looking at him. He was used to being the center of attention but this was peculiar, as were the surroundings. The room was the size of a small airplane hangar. There were no windows and rectangular medical machines filled every conceivable space except for the large metallic cylindrical tubes lining the wall opposite him. And people were everywhere. The people in white clothing moved like a well-trained symphony of musicians, communicating crisply with each movement deliberate and important. *If I'm not dead, where am I?* Panic and fear overwhelmed him. He tried reaching toward the luminescent tubes protruding from him but his arms were heavy as cement. Someone grabbed his arm.

"Daddy, calm down. Everything's okay," said a familiar female voice. It took all his strength to cock his head toward the sound. "Daddy, it's me, Claudia!" *Claudia?*

"You're going to be fine. Trust us," he heard a familiar young man's voice say as deep sleep overpowered him.

He awoke to Baroque music flittering about him. The same unnatural grogginess overwhelmed his senses as did the light. He forced himself up to his elbows and leaned back against the pillows to survey the room. Numerous luminescent tubes still protruded from his arms and body—even his head. The room bore no windows, evoking a claustrophobic feeling. To his left was a white end table and two chairs resting against the wall. Above them hung two unremarkable floral paintings. On the end table a large transparent decanter of water sat next to an empty glass. Next to it were two small aluminum packets. *Looks and smells like a hospital room.* Through the circular window of the room door, he saw people clothed in white surgical masks passing by.

A strange face glanced into the room through the window. He panicked a moment as he heard the click of a lock and watched the door slowly swing open. Filling the doorway was a being that looked like a man, only it wasn't a man. Behind him was a woman. The man entered first and stood at the foot of the bed. Then the woman. When their eyes met, she smiled. She was unnaturally well-built and buxom. She was smaller than the man but had the same kind of face. The texture of their skin and features reminded Williams of a mannequin, yet they appeared to be human beings. *They look like...androids.* Both stood at the foot of the bed, gazing at him with a good-natured yet unnatural smile that was both kindly and unnerving. A loud voice speaking an unfamiliar language preceded someone who sounded decidedly more human. He stood at the front of the doorway while he talked. In his hands, Williams noticed, was a thin rectangular device the size of a large book, which the man touched repeatedly. After one of the taps on the device, a holographic image appeared above it, which the man moved and re-sized repeatedly. He clicked it again with his finger and it was gone.

The people at the foot of the bed deferred with an almost imperceptible nod as the man in the doorway entered the room. He was handsome and young, too young to be a doctor. He grabbed one of the chairs against the wall as he continued talking to someone before tapping his ear-lobe twice with his right index finger. He stood at the left side of the bed offering a wide, becoming smile before sitting down.

"Mr. Williams, before we beginning, we strongly recommending you taking the pills and water. It will ease the lethargy you feeling and clearing you of unseemly grogginess."

"Sir," said the man at the foot of the bed as he motioned with his head toward the decanter of water.

"Oh, yes, quite right. Thanking you," responded the man. "You don't having the energy for that yet, do you? Here, letting me helping you."

Williams gratefully watched as the man poured the water and unwrapped the pills. He placed the tablets in Williams' open hand and pushed it toward his mouth. His face scowled at the taste, causing everyone in the room to chuckle.

"I know the pills are tasting utterly horribleness but the water will soonly eliminating the taste," said the man kindly.

He was right. The sickening metallic taste soon disappeared leaving an aftertaste vaguely reminiscent of tangerines.

"All of it. Trusting us," the man said as he held the glass to Williams' mouth. He obeyed willingly, for with each swallow he felt revived. He drained the glass and motioned for more.

"That's enoughing for now. Giving it a moment Mr. Williams and you will beginning feeling its effects."

"It'll also making the light seem less brighting," said the strange female.

"Yes. Less brighting," offered the man next to her.

The young man cocked his head over his shoulder and leaned toward the beings and said in a low whisper, "We should using late 20th, early 21st century English. He's probably confusing enoughing." The two politely bowed their heads in unison.

"The pills should be taking effect if they haven't already," offered the man, turning back to Williams. He was right. The light of the room was almost instantly tolerable and he found his breathing now free and easy. His grogginess, too, was rapidly dissipating.

"I do feel better."

"Good! Mr. Williams, my name is Doctor Zedekiah Olsen. I'm the chief scientist and administrator of this facility. These are my colleagues, Dr. Binary—he's the male—and Dr. Code."

"Hello," said Williams smiling. "No offense but they look...different."

Olsen chuckled as Binary and Code smiled. "We'll get to that. They're here to help, I assure you."

"Do you know where you are, Mr. Williams?" asked Dr. Binary.

"He's not going to know where he is," Dr. Code interjected.

"Perhaps it's more important to tell you when you are," said Olsen patiently.

"When?" asked Williams.

"The year," offered Dr. Binary.

"Just tell me what's going on, all right?" Williams barked, "And we'll go from there."

"Quite right. Yes," said Olsen as he ran his left hand through his abundant black hair. "Mr. Williams...the year is 2940," he said deliberately, pausing to let it register.

Williams gave no immediate response. A wry smile crossed Williams' face, but it wasn't because of Olsen's statement. Whatever he ingested gave a spike of sexual energy and vigor that surprised him. He hadn't felt such arousal since his mid-fifties.

"The year is 2940?" Williams said, giddy with the newfound potency.

"Yes."

He smiled sarcastically. "And how is that possible?"

Doctors Binary and Code rubbed their hands together in unison. "We can prove it to you."

"Not yet," said Olsen politely, yet sternly. "Mr. Williams, you were cryogenically frozen on July 6, 2002— the day after you 'died.'" Everyone in the room chuckled.

"Why is that funny?" asked Williams tartly.

"Death is humorous to us now. It is no longer a cause for concern. Although accidents do happen now and then."

He now had Williams' full attention. "How did I get here?"

"That's a long story. But what you need to know now is that we found a cure for aging as well as how to 'resurrect' the cryogenically frozen." Olsen leaned in close, then whispered as if he were sharing a secret. "Science discovered the secret to the fountain of youth."

Williams furrowed his brow and gulped. He detected no hint of levity, just earnest seriousness. "A cure for aging? You say that like it was a disease."

"In a very literal way, aging *was* a disease, Mr. Williams. But no more. We've cured it. With the help of some friends."

"How is that possible?"

"How old do you think I am?"

"I don't know—27, 28."

"I'm 477 years old," Dr. Olsen deadpanned.

Williams' jaw slacked. *Could this be real or is this an addled brain's last gasp*? he wondered.

"When I first awoke..." began Williams, feeling more comfortable. Olsen patted him on his left arm gently.

"I think I know what you're going to say."

"Is it time?" asked Dr. Binary. Olsen nodded then tapped his right ear lobe with his finger.

"Send the children in," he said, speaking to the air.

After Claudia and John-Henry left, he laid on the bed staring at the ceiling. Though the fluorescent tubes protruded outward from his entire body, he wasn't in pain, but an astonishing weakness pervaded his being. His body wanted to sleep but his mind raced to the past, reminding him of things done and undone. His "first life," as Claudia called it, was one of accomplishment and notoriety. He'd achieved acclaim and wealth in his Hall of Fame baseball career, and following his retirement, traveled to all the places he dreamed of as a boy while fishing every water hole he fancied.

In his personal life, he was not as successful. But after three divorces, he finally found true love in Louise Kaufmann, with whom he lived blissfully for twenty years until her death. Losing her was devastating. *I wish you were here now, my dear Louise.*

He was relieved to die. Regret engulfed his mind as much as weakness overwhelmed his failing body. He remembered poignantly the sadness he felt for not being a better husband and father. As he closed his eyes for what he thought would be the final time, there was blessed nothingness until the bright light of the hospital room.

The thought of living again scared him. It was unnatural, against the order of things. *Just like this place*, he thought as he carefully grabbed the clamped water tube dangling from the panel behind him. The water refreshed him somewhat, but not the memories that flooded upon him.

While a brash rookie in 1939, he remembered telling a Boston sports reporter his only goal in life was to walk down the street and have people say, "There goes the greatest hitter who ever lived." He accomplished it but found it empty. As his career's end loomed in September 1960, columnist Huck Finnegan wrote a stinging valedictory, saying his career was unprecedented in the "annals of selfishness" as it was his records first, the team second. The memory of Finnegan's words still stung. Years later, while reeling in a tarpon on his boat in the Florida Keys, he admitted to Louise the criticism was true.

The bitter disappointment of never winning a World Series was his only professional regret. He played in only one, batting an embarrassing .200, and with a World Series berth awaiting the winner of playoff games in 1948 and 1949, he floundered. The misery of never winning was made more galling having to watch the New York Yankees win eleven titles during his career. While always on friendly terms with Yankee players, he inwardly resented their success. *Does baseball still exist?* he wondered as he drifted off to sleep.

He sat upright in bed watching the 30th century equivalent of a television. Its 3D holographic projections jolting outward from the wall unnerved him. Claudia reminded him to turn off 3D projection mode by saying "off" or "2D," as it was now calibrated to his voice. He turned it off by barking "off" much louder than the auditory interface required. While watching the TV recede into the wall, an android nurse bolted through the door, asking him if he needed anything. She was easily identifiable as an android as everything she did was mechanical and rote, almost comically so. First, she asked him if he was all right and needed immediate assistance. Then, she offered to walk him to the restroom, then food, then a massage. She finished by puffing his pillows, followed by a strangely suggestive rubbing of his shoulder. Finally, after throwing a programmed smile, she left with the predictable offer of help if he should need anything.

"She's one of the older models," John-Henry told him as the android left the room. "They're regulated to service-oriented jobs now and...'pleasuring functions.' Most of the androids in the hospital are the latest versions. They're sentient. She's not."

News of his resurrection was international news. Williams learned that baseball was now not just an American sport but was enormously popular worldwide, and he was as lionized in the 30th century as he ever was in his first life. Interview requests from the media poured in.

"What would I say to them?" he lamented. "I've got to

get a hold on this."

Claudia rose from the lounge chair against the wall and sat on his bed, careful to avoid sitting on any of the tubes still protruding from his body. She put his left hand in hers.

"Daddy, everything's going to be all right. It really is," she said intently.

"You don't know that."

"Yes, I do! John-Henry and I have been alive again for a little over a year. The shock you're feeling is natural. We felt it, too. But I promise you—I promise you," she said, her blue eyes peering into his as she squeezed his hand, "Everything will be glorious."

Her intensity was riveting. He looked at her a long time to see if he could detect any guile but found none.

"But what am I going to do now?" he mused out loud.

"Daddy, you have unlimited opportunities now that you can't imagine! You can play baseball again, fly, travel, fish, whatever! No one has to worry about money anymore. Anything you want to do, you can!" she said, her voice rising in enthusiasm.

A large gathering of doctors and medical students gathered around him, watching his every move. Never one for niceties, he blurted out, "Is this necessary?"

"We're almost done, Mr. Williams," said Olsen politely smiling.

It would take longer for him to fully resurrect due to the complications that arose during his cryogenic stasis, Dr. Code told him. "Normally it takes three weeks. But it's going to take twelve to fourteen weeks for you. You're in the initial stages of resurrection. Your biological systems are re-booting and need to be stabilized before cellular tissue regeneration."

"You're going to find your coordination uneven during the reanimation phase as well—especially at the beginning," chimed in Dr. Binary. "So please use the cane we provided for you."

"What about athletic ability and eyesight?" asked Williams.

Dr. Olsen puffed his cheeks and shrugged his shoulders as he answered, "It'll return to its normal biological efficacy."

To help him acclimate to the 30th century, John-Henry and Claudia gave him a holoputer, a book-sized plate that was "part-computer, part everything else," they said, and encouraged him to explore the global library records to more fully adapt to this "second life."

"It's designed to interconnect with any global hologram matrix server. So you can take it with you wherever you go," said John-Henry.

"Well, where's the damn 'on' button?"

"It's voice-activated," Claudia said, chuckling.

"Of course, it is. Whatever happened to good old-fashioned buttons," Williams scowled. "On...ON!"

Shafts of reticulated light jutted upward from the pad and coalesced into an attractive female hologram.

"Hello," the image said happily. "I see you haven't calibrated your holoputer yet. Step one, please breathe on the pad. Step two, place any finger on the pad. Step three, look at the pad. Step four, say your name. This will allow the holoputer to calibrate itself to you via DNA mapping and retinal biometric certification," the sultry voice of the holographic image said.

The image of the woman waited as programmed, first putting her hands on her ample hips, then throwing her long black hair seductively backward.

"What the...?" Williams said, amused.

"Shall I repeat the steps?" said the holographic woman, putting her right index finger's tip into her teeth.

"The image was one surmised from your background," said Dr. Code. "I hope it's pleasing."

"It's fine," Williams said, ignoring the suggestion as he put his thumb on the pad.

"Now state your name, please," said the hologram.

"Ted. Williams."

"Say again, please."

"Ted. WILLIAMS."

"Again, please."

"TED. F-ING. WILLIAMS!" he barked in frustration.

"Thank you, Mr. Ted. F-ing. Williams," the hologram replied with a seductive wink.

"No! Just Ted Williams," Claudia snickered.

"Apologies. Mr. Ted Williams," said the hologram with a sultry smile. "Connection to the global historical archive matrix servers has been initiated. You are now calibrated and connected to use this holoputer at your convenience, Mr. Ted Williams."

"Global historical archive matrix servers?"

"Think of it as this century's internet," Dr. Code said.

This was a different world. Mankind had made incredible technological advances since his death. Interstellar travel was now possible with the advent of light-speed capable ships. Trips to the moon, Mars,

Neptune, and nearby dwarf planets Pluto and Makemake were now as routine as a flight to Detroit in his day. Inter-global travel as well was astonishingly fast. Most global destinations were now only a ten to fifteen flight. Williams watched and listened enrapt as the holoputer's narrator said it took more time planning a trip than actually taking it.

Other technologies that had been in their infancy when he died were now commonplace. Quantum evolutionary leaps spanned every conceivable discipline. Water-, compressed air- and solar-powered engines replaced the internal combustion engine of the 21st century. Advances in computerization, metallurgy, robotics, aerodynamics, agriculture, pedagogy, and terra-forming that were the thing of science fiction in his lifetime were fundamental to 30th-century life. Medical technology, too, had far outstripped the achievements of his day. DNA reprogramming, artificial organs, synthesized blood, and nanobots programmed to eradicate disease-causing cells were all mainstream. Diseases like Alzheimer's, cancer, heart disease, and diabetes were now relegated to historical medical events. Even a cure for baldness had been discovered.

Williams activated the auditory pulse interface on his ear to call the android. He asked for a sandwich and the orange smoothie that Dr. Olsen told him were foundational to his reanimation period. He hated its taste but did as he was told. He was already able to walk so it must be working, he thought to himself as he ambled his way to the bathroom. After flushing the toilet, he caught a glimpse of himself in the mirror. He looked like he did in his early fifties. His skin was taut and flush. His vision, too, was much improved compared to when he first awoke. His energy levels were surprising as well. For the first time since awakening in the Alcor storage hangar, he felt excitement. *Could this all be really happening?* He vigorously walked back to his bed and un-paused the holoputer. He wanted to know everything that had happened while he was cryogenically frozen. Something strange coursed through him, too. Something he hadn't felt in the later years of his first life. Hope.

Massive political upheaval had also occurred, he learned. The secret society behind most of the 20th and early 21st centuries crimes was uncovered and its perpetrators executed. As part of a plea deal, one of the society's members showed *prima facie* evidence of the cabal's work, including the fraudulent passage of the 16th Amendment, the assassination of the Kennedy brothers and Martin Luther King, the orchestration of the September 11 attacks by George W. Bush and Dick Cheney, the treasonous Barack Obama and Joe Biden presidencies, the criminality of Bill and Hillary Clinton, the Antifa Berkeley Massacre of 2025, the Rockefeller Banking Conspiracy, and the numerous Big Oil and Big Pharma crimes.

By 2028, Williams learned, the Muslims' infiltration of Europe and America in geographically strategic cities was complete. On Christmas Day, 2028, the Muslims, Marxists, and Russians attacked the eastern seaboard of the U.S. and England while the Chinese and N. Koreans attacked the west coast of America. Aided by traitors within the U.S. government, the Mus-Rus-Socialist alliance, or MRS as it was called, made significant headway into the U.S. overtaking the eastern seaboard from Maine to Florida and the entire west coast. Washington, D.C., San Francisco, and New York all fell. The Freemen Alliance, as they called themselves, was teetering on collapse but after regrouping, swore on the memory of the American Founding Fathers, that they would repel the invaders. They succeeded, Williams was happy to learn.

After nearly fifteen years of fighting, the MRS and Freemen struck a peace accord. America was divided up with the eastern seaboard and west coast states, as well as Michigan and Wisconsin, going to the MRS. The Freemen agreed to take Canada, Mexico, Central America, Brazil, the Rocky Mountain states, the American south and the Midwest as well as Alaska. The Hawaiian Islands went to the MRS except for the island of Kauai, which was ceded to the Freemen by the MRS as a final gesture of peace. Europe, eastern Russia, Turkey, Egypt, Israel, Japan, Micronesia, New Zealand, and Australia were also designated Freemen territory. The rest of the world belonged to the MRS. Independence, Missouri was designated the capital of the Freemen Alliance while Havana, Cuba became the capital of the MRS. Washington, D.C. was christened neutral territory and became the western hemisphere's Geneva, Williams discovered.

While peace had finally come, the nuclear fallout had turned parts of the world into a wasteland. That was when the Proximas and Zarisians made their first appearance. Williams paused the holoputer. The offhand comment by Olsen regarding the curing of aging "with the help of some friends" now made sense. He took a bite of the sandwich then un-paused the holoputer. He learned that on July 4th, 2040, a Proximan command ship landed on the Washington Mall just east of the rebuilt Washington

Monument. They already spoke fluent English as well as Mandarin, Arabic, and Russian, the dominant languages of Earth. They pledged to help rebuild the planet's damaged atmosphere and ecosystem in return for the world sharing its collective literature, music and historical records.

It was fascinating reading about the Proximas and the Zarisians. Extraterrestrial beings were the subject of much speculation in his time but now in the 30th century, it was unremarkable. He learned that the Proximas came from the Proxima Centauri B star solar system, a scant 4.6 light-years away from Earth. Early 21st-century man thought it a dead zone planet due to its smaller sun, as it was thought to strip it of vital life-giving atmosphere, but they were wrong. A flourishing civilization lived there even more advanced than Earth. The Proximas, as they preferred to be called, were a bipedal humanoid species. It was they who were the source of untold stories of alien visitations and sightings, Williams learned. Their horizontal eye-drop black eyes, green skin, oblong head and diminutive stature were at first unsettling to humans, but their generosity and mild natures eventually won over even the most ardent anti-terrestrials. It was almost too fanciful to believe, he thought as he chugged down the rest of the smoothie. He threw the smoothie container into a trash receptacle adjacent his bed and watched it disintegrate into a small yellow cube. He then flicked the hologram projection array for more information on the Proximas.

The Proximas knew of Earth as many millennia before they mapped out the Terran solar system, he learned. But while traveling to Neptune on a routine mining expedition discovered a sentient, albeit unevolved, species. Thenceforth, they closely monitored Earth and waited patiently until humans evolved. Given the devastation of World War III, and believing humans as a species that possessed great potential, the Proximas and Zarisians mutually agreed to make themselves known. Eventually, after four hundred years of cultural exchange, the "Earthens," as they called humans, had earned their trust, and it was then that the Zarisians and Proximas shared their biogerontology science, effectively giving humankind the missing scientific pieces that made biological immortality possible.

The Zarisians were long-standing allies of the Proximas and like them, surveyed Earth for hundreds of years while they learned the dominant languages of the planet and watched humankind's societal evolution. Zarisians, he discovered, came from a planet called Zarisia, which was in the same solar system as Proxima Centauri B. Scientists in April 2019, Williams read eagerly, had detected another exoplanet in the same solar system shared by the Proximas. Zarisia, or what human scientists called Proxima C, was supposedly a frigid planet inhospitable for life. What humans didn't know was that protective shielding far beyond the ken of 21st-century man had hidden the planet's civilization from Earth's astronomers. Another intriguing fact Williams discovered was that unlike the Proximas, the Zarisians were, except for their skin, virtually identical to humans, biologically. Other than a stronger immune system and superior resistance to cold temperatures, Zarisians and humans were so compatible that intermarriage between the species became commonplace. Williams let out a laugh as the female narrator said Zarisian women were highly desirable as companions to Earthens given their buxom figures. It wasn't the only thing that was intriguing to humans, Williams learned. Many on Earth called the Zarisians the "Palindromes" as their native planetary language was almost entirely made up of palindromic sentencing. Zarisian surnames, too, were unique as they started with a number. He chuckled at the thought.

After the bio-fluorescent tubes had been removed, which Binary and Code assured him was a significant step forward to his full resurrection, John-Henry and Claudia escorted him to the roof of the hospital. Williams was surprised to see a garden growing atop the building. He stepped onto the balcony into the cool desert air and looked up at the full moon hovering in the early evening sky. He thought of Louise. He remembered fishing in the Keys at dusk with her while they shared a similar sky. It was a different moon then. Even without a telescope, he could clearly see buildings on its surface. Over seven million people lived there now. There was even a university there that specialized in mining science, Claudia told him. Blackbirds squawked at each other from a nearby mesquite tree, disturbing his reverie. He was still lonely for Louise but felt buoyed by another chance at life. And Claudia and John-Henry were with him now.

In the final stages of the reanimation cycle, Williams could scarcely believe the changes in his body. He looked like he did while in the full flowering of his youth in the 1940s. Binary and Code told him he was biologically twenty-eight years old as confirmed by what they called "cell resonance." He would need to re-build his muscles through careful weight training, and there would be bouts of insomnia, Olsen warned, but the process was complete. All who underwent the reanimation procedure would also have to come back once a year for a homeostasis checkup, Binary strongly reminded him. It was a small price to pay for immortality.

On his last day at the facility, the staff threw a party for him. He was their most famous patient, he was told repeatedly. Many asked for autographs, even the sentient androids. Some of the female Zarisians and human nurses offered other pleasures. While talking to two female Zarisian doctors as he ate a piece of chocolate cake, he saw himself in the mirror embedded in the wall. A rosy glow filled his cheeks and there were no more gray hairs or age spots on his arms and face. His eyesight, too, was as keen as it had ever been in his first life, and his energy levels were what he remembered from his youth. He excused himself and made his way to the roof garden. As he sat on a bench next to rosemary and lavender bushes, he thought of what was to come.

He would learn from the mistakes of his past, he determined. He would not waste this opportunity, this new life. He wasn't sure what he would do, but knew he wanted something beyond professional accomplishment, something of meaning and purpose. Now, he had a second chance at life, and this time, he would do things right. Now when he walked down the street, he wanted people to say, "There goes a great father and grandfather...and man."

He recalled the conversation with Claudia when he first awoke from cryogenic stasis. "Everything will be glorious...you have unlimited opportunities now that you can't imagine!" She was right, and those possibilities enthralled him.

He still loved baseball. *But should I try to play again?* he wondered. Spring training for the new season was still eight months away. Plus, the regret of never winning a World Series still hung in his mind like a specter, ever reminding him of his failure. But now, it was possible again. Numerous teams around the globe, and even from teams on Mars and the moon, reached out to him offering a tryout. Even the Yankees. But there were other things he wanted to do first. After watching the July 1969 moon landing, and space television shows of the time, he remembered fantasizing about flying in space, of visiting other planets. He was a trained pilot after all, having flown fighter jets in World War II and Korea. Claudia and John-Henry encouraged him to apply to the flight training program in Mexico, as did the hospital staff. No, he decided. First, he would travel.

After leaving the hospital, he and the children flew to the moon, where he was asked to make the ceremonial first pitch in a game between the Moon Bots and the Boston Red Sox, his old team from his first life. They then went to Neptune and Pluto, then to Zarisia and Proxima. While hiking Zarisia's equivalent of the Grand Canyon, the Epis Gorge, he told the children he wanted to play baseball again. He knew he'd be an oddity at first, but he didn't care. After a tryout, the Utah Dinos of the North American National League signed him. Boston made an offer out of courtesy to his achievements, but he rejected it. In this second life, he wanted a fresh start. And that meant a new city.

It didn't take long to re-build his strength. After a few months of work in the gym and under Dr. Code's careful supervision, he was stronger than he was in his twenties.

"Are you sure you want to do this, Dad?" John-Henry asked him.

"What else am I going to do?"

"Dad!" Claudia bit back.

"I know what you're going to say. And you're right. It doesn't matter to me what I do, just as long as you two are with me," he replied.

A meaningful silence hung in the air between them. Claudia, then John-Henry, hugged him, and he them. *Things will be different this time.*

Looking out through the shuttle craft's passenger window, Williams gaped at the massive crowd of well-wishers and media that awaited him at the Dinos' spring training facility in Surprise, Arizona. A rush of panic grabbed him at almost the same moment the shuttle craft's landing gear touched down upon the cement.

"What are you nervous about? This is a great day, and your children are waiting for you at the landing site. See?" Code said, motioning with her head toward the window.

Claudia waved at him enthusiastically but all he could offer was a weak smile in reply.

Code leaned over to his ear and whispered, "Deep breaths. You'll be fine."

But it did nothing to ease the sudden nausea filling his stomach. Everyone stood but him as the whirring sound of the engine gradually dissipated. *Can I do this?* Code and Binary exited, slinging their day bags over their shoulders.

"All clear, sir," shouted Code, feigning her best security mien as she waited for him by the door. Binary took the cue and joined her in the charade.

"Yes, all clear, dude...I mean sir," offered Binary,

spawning a full-bodied laugh from Williams. They did know how to make him relax.

"You two are kind of over-qualified for security work, aren't you?" John-Henry asked them with a wink as he shook Binary's hand.

"Happy to do it," smiled Code. "Besides, your father and I are special friends now." A long beat passed between them, punctuated by knowing smiles among all but Williams.

"They're waiting for us," he weakly offered, hoping to change the subject. As they made their way to the makeshift podium for the press conference, Claudia saw his face flush red as a wry smile crossed his face.

"Are you blushing, Dad?"

"There'll be none of that," he replied, as John-Henry broke out laughing.

A number of Dinos' officials awaited them as they approached the dais. He listened quietly as the general manager and team owner praised his once-stellar Hall of Fame career and how happy they were to sign him. He was once uncomfortable with such shows of praise, but time, death, and resurrection had refined him. He found himself genuinely appreciative of the effort made to make him feel comfortable. As he stepped to the dais, he shot a glance back at Code and Binary who gave him a thumbs-up sign. He fumbled with his bowtie for a moment out of a psychological need for comfort. He was not the only one wearing one, he saw. Fashion from the 21st century was all the rage, he discovered. Almost everyone was wearing one, even some of the women. He was also pleased the fedora had made a comeback too, and happily donned it for the occasion.

"I don't have any prepared comments," he quietly said. "But I do want to say thank you to the general manager and the owner for this lovely welcome. It means a lot."

Shouts and clapping of acclimation drowned his ears. As the din subsided, a lithe blonde reporter caught his attention.

"Mr. Williams," she shouted, "What are your thoughts as you embark on your career as a baseball player again? Do you think you can still play as well as you did in your first life?"

"Yes. I wouldn't have signed otherwise."

"Do you think you'll be as good a hitter as you were with the Red Sox?" another reporter asked.

"The game is different," he said as he ran his hands over his chin before re-donning the fedora. "But I know I can still play—and hit—like I did before."

He took a deep breath as he walked down the corridor to the players' clubhouse. Framed pictures and holographic projections of stars from yesteryear lined the corridor. He suddenly felt overwhelmed with insecurity and fear. *I'm just an oddity*, he thought as he leaned up against the cement wall. For a moment he wished he were back at the hospital.

"What you're feeling is normal," said a male voice out of the darkness to his left.

He could hear the clip clap of rubberized spikes caressing the concrete as the voice approached him. A young man with a shock of orange-red hair cascading out of his Dinos' baseball hat finally came out of the diffused gray light. He was in his mid-twenties with a squatty, endomorphic body type. *Probably a catcher.*

"I went through the cryogenic process in the late 22nd century and was resurrected two years ago. I think I know a little of what you're going through. I'm Larry Oldenburg," said the man as he extended his right hand. Williams gratefully shook it.

"I'm Ted. Thank you for that. I appreciate it."

"You were my baseball hero growing up—I probably shouldn't say that," the man said, smiling.

"Please don't," Williams said, half-serious.

"Sorry," Larry said, pursing his lips. "Can I ask you something?"

Williams shook his head once downward in reply.

"Why do you want to do this again?"

"Why did you?"

"Because I love the game. And unfinished business."

"Me too," Williams said, looking at the ground.

"Because you never won a World Series?" A long pause drifted between them.

"Yes."

Larry pursed his lips in an upside-down smile while cocking his head up and down repeatedly in understanding.

"We have a good team here. We have a real shot at a title. I'm serious. If you hit as well as you did in your heyday, I think we'll get there."

As Williams entered the clubhouse, any remaining insecurity he felt was destroyed by the warm welcome of the players. Many asked for autographs, even the stars on the team. He had made it a point to tell the general manager and owner that he didn't want any special favors. They ignored his wishes, Williams noticed, as he was given the best stall in the clubhouse. He did afford himself one luxury—he asked for the number nine he wore with the Red Sox. He laughed heartily as a young shortstop who already wore the number agreed to give it to him in return for an autographed bat and a date with Claudia.

Due to his proclivity to pull the baseball to right field, the Cleveland manager Lou Boudreau came upon a scheme to thwart Williams' hitting. He put all the infielders to the right side of the field and strategically placed one in short right field where many of Williams' line drives fell. The "Williams Shift," as it came to be called, was a brilliant strategy that more teams adopted against him. His stubbornness in changing his approach at the plate hurt his career, he knew. One writer of his time said his reluctance to change cost him over ten points to his lifetime batting average of .344. This time, he resolved, he would be an all-field hitter. After signing with the Dinos, Dr. Olsen arranged for him to use the hospital's holo room where new doctors honed their skills with holograms and obsolete androids. Code wrote a software holo-program that emulated actual ballparks. The technology was remarkable. Other than minor pixilation in the sky, it was as if he was standing in a real stadium. It became an indispensable tool in honing his new all-field approach to hitting. He practiced for hours hitting off a batting tee to develop the necessary muscle memory. Sometimes some of the hospital staff would come in and sit in the holographic stands to watch, especially Code. She never missed a training session, he noticed.

After arriving at spring training, he honed his new approach in live batting practice. And it worked. He was no longer a dead-pull left-handed hitter. He hit .365 in spring training with half of his homeruns going out of left field.

After the last Spring Training game, reporters swarmed him at his locker in the player's clubhouse, peppering him with questions on his new hitting style. They also couldn't resist delving into personal questions, Williams noticed. "Who are you dating?" asked one. "What is your favorite part of your second life?" asked another. Reporters hadn't changed much from his time, he mused to himself after they finally left as he grabbed a few remaining personal items from his locker. Most journalists and analysts predicted he wouldn't be able to compete in a new age of baseball. Some were even bold enough to ask him face-to-face. It rankled him, but John-Henry and Claudia, and even Code, told him to use it as motivational fuel. Yes, the game had changed from his time, he patiently explained to one pesky reporter, but so had he. And it was still baseball.

The hotel door closed behind him as he flopped his luggage heavily on the queen-sized bed. He pushed the heavy burgundy curtains to the sides from the window and looked through it below to Central Park. A light autumn fog hovered above the trees like an interested ghost, as warmly-dressed passersby mingled through the walkways. As he looked west across the park, lavender and orange clouds obscured the setting sun. Its beauty enthralled him. *Life is a gift.* He was never sentimental or reflective in his first life, yet something had changed in him since his resurrection. Maybe it was being with the children again. Or just having a second chance at life. But something else happened that he didn't expect—he'd fallen in love with Code and she with him. At first, he felt he was betraying Louise somehow. *But what could I have done?*

She's gone. Claudia told him she would want him to be happy and move on with his life. In the past he would've pushed her away for coming too close to his heart. But not now.

His mind raced through all the other happenings of the past year. He loved playing ball again, but it didn't surpass the joy he felt being with his children or Code. Still, he mused, as a crooked smile creased his face, it had been a gratifying season. The Dinos had captured the National League pennant by seven games and he'd led the league in hits, on-base percentage, average and RBIs. And his play against the Dodgers in the League Championship Series had earned him the League Champion Series MVP Award. Now his Dinos would face the dreaded Yankees in the Fall Classic. A combination of nervous tension and excitement wrestled within him at the prospect. It was a chance at the redemption he had longed for in his first life.

He was jolted from his daydreaming by his holoputer chiming with the strike of the hour as it rested inside his brown leather bag. He remembered the night Code gave it to him. In Zarisian culture, he learned, it was customary for those having a birthday to gift someone close to them. It was one of the many things he had come to love about Zarisians, and her.

"Knowing when to lay something down and to pick it up again is wisdom," she had said, her face sparkling as she handed it to him. "Maybe this bag will help."

"Is that an old Zarisian proverb?" he'd asked, his eyes aglow with love.

"Yes. From our equivalent of your Benjamin Franklin," she'd said as they kissed.

Beating the Yankees in seven games in the 2941 World Series was the first championship he would enjoy. Over the next ten seasons, he would win his first Gold Glove Award, Silver Sluggers, and more season MVPs. He would retire with 4,805 hits and 807 homeruns. No other hitter, not even Babe Ruth or the Zarisian Zanaz 9-Tuylze, could match his output of both average and power.

For the second time, he was voted into the Hall of Fame, but this time his family was with him at the induction ceremony. As he made his way to the podium after his name was announced, a cavalcade of memories flooded forth. He thought of that fabled game seven in the 2941 Series that had become legendary. It was the single greatest moment in his entire career, first or second life. Writer John Updike's *New Yorker* valedictory article, "Hub Fans Bid Kid Adieu" filled his memory and emotions. There was one sentence from the piece he never forgot: "Therefore the last time in all eternity that their regular left fielder...would play..." Updike's extraneous comment "the last time in all eternity" evoked a wry smile again as he prepared for that final at bat.

He remembered pawing at the earth with his left foot while waiting for the Yankees' pitcher when somehow, out of the ether, Huck Finnegan's barbed words bubbled up. He wished Finnegan could've been there to witness what came next. In the bottom of the eleventh, in game seven, on the second pitch of the at bat, he hit a hanging slider over the left-field fence for a series-clinching home run. *I wonder what Finnegan and Updike would think of this*? he thought as he rounded the bases.

Years later, he thought the same thing as he arrived at the podium to give his second Hall of Fame induction speech. Emotion stopped him from speaking as he looked out over the crowd. Holographic images of former baseball greats projected on the Hall of Fame building behind him. Many of them he had known and played with: Joe DiMaggio, Mickey Mantle, Yogi Berra, and others. With a start he realized the sepia-toned Yankees of yore were no longer enemies, but friends. Friends with whom he now carried an equal weight in the balances of baseball immortality. He looked out over the crowd again. His family filled the first few rows, and friends and fans the others. *Life is very beautiful.*

The crowd spontaneously cheered him, giving him a moment. As he composed himself, he recounted fondly to the crowd the new joy he had found in baseball. And in life. He recounted in detail the hitting of that fabled homerun, and the sweet remembrance at the Dinos' fans uproarious, unhinged joy as he rounded the bases. It was their first championship as it was his. "The Homerun of Redemption," the media called it. It was the first championship for his friend and teammate Larry Oldenburg, too. He was the first to embrace him at home plate as his other teammates swarmed them. They would win nine more World Series championships together, but none would be as fulfilling.

Having accomplished all he could as a baseball player, the stars beckoned to him. He went to pilot school. It was a rigorous five-year program, but he was as determined to become a space pilot as he was a great baseball player. After graduating, he became a shuttle pilot for a time but eventually bought his own ship, which he and Code used to travel the known galaxy and beyond. They explored hundreds of planets while charting flight paths that crisscrossed the Milky Way. In time, he became as honored as a pilot and adventurer as he was a baseball player.

Time passed. His wanderlust fulfilled, he and Code bought homes on Zarisia and Earth—Utah and Italy—and raised their ever-growing family. Other hobbies were taken up, including painting and drawing. He even toyed with acting and police work, and was often asked to coach and manage baseball, but the gravitational pull of home and family precluded such engagement.

Not that there weren't other adventures. Many were unforgettable. He fished the coral reefs of the southern continent of Zarisia; watched the cloned, legendary racehorse Secretariat run the Belmont Stakes; scaled the Meteora rock pillars in Greece; hiked Yosemite in California; and scuba dove with great whites near Guadalupe Island in Mexico.

In the years of his existence, he had achieved every goal and adventure he had desired and had tasted the full spectrum of the human experience, even death. But now, he determined, those unexpected extra innings needed to end. He had exited previously with an empty heart but now his heart was fulfilled. This time, he would go on his terms, not on the whim of indifferent nature. And this time it would be forever. And so, on the seven hundredth birthday of his second life, Ted Williams, the greatest hitter who ever lived, deliberately ended that gift of eternal life while surrounded by thirty-five generations of descendants. This time his remains were cremated and scattered over the Florida Keys by his beloved Claudia, John-Henry, and Code. This time he would not return. And this time, he passed in peace.

ACKNOWLEDGMENTS

I've only had three teachers in my life who made an impact upon me and all were in the English Department at Weber State University. First, I want to thank Dr. Douglas M. Spainhower for teaching me the rudiments of English punctuation and grammar during my freshman year. He made it come alive and more importantly made it memorable. I still cannot think of a colon without his comparing it to talk show host Johnny Carson. And to Dr. Gerald R. Grove who encouraged me to become an English major and to write. And lastly, to Dr. Gordon T. Allred, whose compliments, encouragement and gentlemanly spirit I will always treasure.

ABOUT ATMOSPHERE PRESS

Atmosphere Press is an independent, full-service publisher for excellent books in all genres and for all audiences. Learn more about what we do at atmospherepress.com.

We encourage you to check out some of Atmosphere's latest releases, which are available at Amazon.com and via order from your local bookstore:

The Short Life of Raven Monroe, a novel by Shan Wee

Insight and Suitability, a novel by James Wollak

It Starts When You Stop, a novel by Johnny Abboud

Orange City, a novel by Lee Matthew Goldberg

Late Magnolias, a novel by Hannah Paige

No Way Out, a novel by Betty R. Wall

The Saint of Lost Causes, a novel by Carly Schorman

Monking Around, a novel by Keith Howchi Kilburn

The Cuckoo of Awareness, a novel by Andrew Brush

The House of Clocks, a novel by Fred Caron

The Tattered Black Book, a novel by Lexy Duck

All Things in Time, a novel by Sue Buyer

American Genes, a novel by Kirby Nielsen

Newer Testaments, a novel by Philip Brunetti

Hobson's Mischief, a novel by Caitlin Decatur

The Red Castle, a novel by Noah Verhoeff

The Farthing Quest, a novella by Casey Bruce